SKELMERSDALE

FICTION RESERVE STOCK 60

AUTHOR

BRYAN, J.

CLASS

AFG

TITLE

Bernard and the cloth monkey

Judith Bryan

grew up in London with a Jamaican and Guyanese heritage. She is a social worker by profession and has one young son. *Bernard and the Cloth Monkey*, her first novel, won the 1997 Saga Prize, an award for unpublished black novelists.

THE SAGA PRIZE

The SAGA Prize was founded in 1994 by author and actress Marsha Hunt to encourage unpublished Black novelists born in the UK and the Republic of Ireland. Sponsored by the SAGA Group, the award is £3000 plus publication of the winning manuscript. Previous winners are *Sister Josephine* by Joanna Traynor (Bloomsbury 1997) and *Some Kind of Black* by Diran Adebayo (Virago 1996).

JUDITH BRYAN

*Bernard and the
Cloth Monkey*

Flamingo
An Imprint of HarperCollins*Publishers*

08089102

Flamingo
An Imprint of HarperCollins*Publishers*
77–85 Fulham Palace Road,
Hammersmith, London W6 8JB

www.**fire**and**water**.com

Published by Flamingo 1999

9 8 7 6 5 4 3 2 1

First published by Flamingo 1998

This novel is a work of fiction. The names,
characters and incidents portrayed in it are the work of the
author's imagination. Any resemblance to actual persons,
living or dead, events or localities, is entirely coincidental.

ISBN 0 00 655196 3

Printed and bound by
Caledonian International Book Manufacturing Ltd, Glasgow

This book is dedicated to:

Those who would be good
Those who would be more
And to those who do go lightly

With thanks to Fishbone Writers, the City Lit, Carol Russell, Geraint Edwards, Bill and Caro and my friends at Orchardton House, and the Bryan family, especially Gladstone and Gloria.

1

The Story Ends

'Beth!'

Suddenly she was awake. The voice was strident, strangled. She lay in bed for several seconds as the light on the landing was switched on, outlining the bedroom door with a thin strip of yellow. There was a scrambling sound, then the thump of a body falling, rising and falling once more.

'No. No, not again,' she whispered. 'Mummy . . .'

Then came the slap of her mother's palm against the door, her voice strong and clear. 'Beth, help me with your Dad.' And she remembered where she was, and why, and that it was not Mummy in trouble but Daddy.

She leaped out of bed and peered into the hallway. Her father lay face down in an angular heap beside the open toilet door. Mummy had him by the shoulders and was trying to lift him, grunting with the effort. Beads of sweat appeared across her forehead and upper lip. She brushed a hand hurriedly along her hairline. With her next movement, and a sharp intake of breath, she managed to sit him up. Her fingers gripped his armpits so that his arms stuck out like a marion-.ette's. His head rolled and flopped; as it fell backward Beth saw just how thin he had become. His eyes, sunken way back into their sockets, appeared as enormous shadows in his face, matched only by the twin tunnels of his nostrils. His skin was paper dry, his lips grey, and deep lines scored his cheeks from nose to chin.

He's really dying. Shocked into action, and without stopping to dwell on his skeletal chest pushing ridges up through his pyjama top, Beth stooped and put her arms around him.

'One, two, three,' said Mummy, and in one movement they dragged him to his feet. She was surprised at how heavy he was still. With an arm around each of their shoulders, he stumbled toward the bedroom he and his wife had shared for twenty-five years. Just as they passed through the doorway he stopped and, with a strangled cry, tried to swing himself about. He clawed the air with his hands, almost upsetting their balance. Beth buckled under his full weight.

'What's the matter?' she asked, sure her mother could interpret his gasping moans.

'Oh God, he wants to use the toilet, that's why he got out of bed. Bernard. B. You're too weak, man. You can have the bed-pan.'

With a violent effort of will he shook his head and said, distinctly, 'No, no, toilet, toilet.' His face contorted with rage.

'What shall we do?'

'Well, he's up now. We may as well take him. You're so proud,' she said, a strange pride in her own voice. They lurched around in the narrow space. Beth winced as his wrists and knuckles rapped against the door jamb.

'OK,' Mummy said, 'come on, B, try to walk, that's right.'

It seemed an eternity before they got back to the toilet.

Mummy kicked at the partially open door and helped manoeuvre him into the tiny square room.

'What now?'

With one hand Mummy lifted the toilet lid and switched on the light. The 100 watt glare was not kind; Bernard's haggard face dropped, his chin resting on his chest. A thin line of spittle dribbled out of his mouth. 'Help me,' said Mummy. They inched his pyjama cord loose and let the trousers fall around his ankles. His private parts hung withered and black, speckled with grey hair, like an empty leather pouch between his liquorice-stick legs. He gave a long sigh and began to urinate.

'Quickly!' Beth screamed, overcome by a sudden, disproportionate panic. Neatly, Mummy rapped her knuckles into the backs of Daddy's knees, and he sat, hard, on the seat. He seemed to fold in on himself then, his hands meek, harmless, in his lap. His shoulders hunched in a way she could not have imagined before now. The sporadic trickle of urine continued for several minutes as he sat without moving or raising his head. Beth and her mother watched him silently, keeping their thoughts to themselves.

'He's really dying,' Beth said eventually, thinking he was asleep.

'Yes,' said Mummy. Then several perfect tears dropped, one by one, from his left eye.

'I'm sorry,' he said, the words unmistakable although his voice was thick with sickness. 'Please, I'm so sorry.'

'Free,' Beth whispered, closing the book on her lap and leaning forward to look at his face. 'It won't be long now, then we'll all be free. You as well, Daddy.'

She let the heavy volume drop to the ground, watching his face for any sign that he had registered the noise. There was none. His skin had settled into an ashy grey colour now he could no longer get up, as if he were literally fading before her eyes. His own eyes roved continuously behind their closed lids, reflecting his frantic dreams. His nostrils were often full of a yellowish, foul-smelling mucus which Mummy wiped away with wadded tissues and oil-dampened flannels, cleaning his face as tenderly as a baby's. The deep grooves on either side of his nose gave him the appearance of a puppet, as did his open mouth, free of its upper teeth which lay in a dish of water on top of the bedside cabinet. He no longer twisted in the sheets, sending bedclothes one way, his body the next. He did not require feeding or watering, unable to swallow now, oblivious to hunger. He needed very little care; the occasional bed-pan, and the frequent removal of nasal mucus, both of which his wife attended to. It was Beth's job to moisten his lips with a little water from time to time, to prevent them from cracking under the dry heat of his rasping breath. And her job to watch. To make sure he did not die alone.

Below his ravaged, gargoyle-like head his body seemed hardly to be there. Her mother had laid him out straight, as if ready for his coffin: feet side by side, hands folded neatly over his stomach, on top of the bedclothes. Apart from the slight hill of feet, the tidy brown parcel of hands, and the steady rise and fall of his chest, he made no significant impression in the bed.

'How the mighty have fallen,' Beth said out loud. He had been a big man, a giant to her as a child. He strode through their world, creating havoc and awe in equal measure. Sometimes distant, disinterested, at other times full of a kind of reckless bonhomie. The very fact that his moods could not be predicted had terrified Beth. He rendered her foolish and he did not suffer fools gladly. He had been sure and assertive in everything he did. And now he depended on them completely; Daddy in the guise of dying old man.

Beth had hardly been aware of the transition. For years he had seemed the same. Until the day she had seen him at the kitchen table, resting one arm on the table top, the other on the back of his chair. His wrists had hung bony from his shirt-sleeves, and he had squinted with pain as he struggled to catch his breath. She had turned away then, unprepared for the sudden pity she felt. She would not turn away anymore.

'It's alright, Daddy,' she said now. 'I'm right here.'

First she noticed the movement of his chest become erratic, then he opened his mouth and drew in a sudden breath. Hoping, still, for that last speech from his death bed, she threw herself to her knees beside him.

'Dad?'

His breath sounded like pebbles stirred in a shallow stream: unfamiliar, increasingly dry and grating. Beth heard her mother's footfall in the downstairs hall.

'Mum,' she yelled, eyes fixed on her father's mouth, 'come quick, his breathing's changed.'

In a moment she was there, resting a warm hand on Beth's shoulder as she too peered into his face. After a while she said, 'Yes, he's gone.'

When, thought Beth, was the precise moment? How did I miss it? I was right here. I was watching, listening.

'Are you sure?' she said. Silence. 'Mum?'

She turned around to find Mummy rinsing his dentures with fresh water from a glass. Without speaking, she pushed

Beth gently away and began to force the teeth between her husband's collapsed lips. She moved them aside, lifeless, rubbery, jamming the dentures against his gums. Water trailed from the plate and smeared over his mouth and chin. Beth was sure she heard a faint complaining moan from Daddy's throat.

'What are you *doing*?'

'If I don't put them in now his mouth will go out of shape, and they won't be able to get them in later.' She was already thinking of the undertakers, the lying-in-state, the funeral. The overwhelming need to keep up appearances.

2

A Right Royal Family

Once upon a time there was an African prince and his beautiful new bride. They lived on an island where there was no food and no water and all the people dressed in rags. Every day the prince's bride, who was now a princess, looked out of her window and saw the people in their rags. She saw all the little children crying, with their tummies puffed up like big balloons because they were hungry. She saw the animals lying dead in the street and the old women with flies sitting on their faces that they couldn't even be bothered to brush off. All day long the men of the island used to jump about and sing and never did any work. And the princess got fed up looking at all this and she said to her husband the prince:

'My husband, we must leave this place. I don't want my children to have big bellies. I don't want the flies on my face when I get old.'

'OK, you're right,' said the prince. 'For, truly, this is a benighted island and all the islands round here are the same. Let's go to England.'

So they packed up all their things, which wasn't much, and got on a boat made of bananas, because those were the only kind strong enough to carry them all the way to England.

The prince and princess liked it in England. They got used to the cold and bought themselves good winter coats and two pairs of galoshes each. And they had lots to eat and lots to drink and they were happy.

One day the princess said to the prince, 'Husband, I would like to have a baby now.' And again he said OK, because she always had good ideas. And very soon the princess gave birth to a lovely baby girl.

It is always the job of an African prince to name the babies. He has to go to the end of the garden, right up to the fence, under the apple tree, and hold the baby up in the air and say Kunta Kinte, very quickly so the baby doesn't get cold. Then he must rush indoors and wrap the baby up and say whatever name comes into his head first. And the prince said, 'Let us call her Elizabeth, after the Queen, because we have been so happy since we came to England.'

'OK,' said his wife, 'but let's change it to Lisa-Beth, and call her Beth, for short.'

Less than one year later, the princess gave birth to twin girls, and they were lovely too. This time, the prince and princess agreed to call the babies Margaret and Anne, after the English princesses, it didn't matter that they were auntie and niece, they were the royal girls. But because they liked names that were a little bit different, they changed the names to Margareta and Anita. That way they could call the twins Greta and Nita, which was really unusual, and no one else at school would have those names.

Really quickly, before you could turn around, the babies started crawling, and then they went to infant school and then to juniors. And they were all very clever and very pretty. They always did as they were told and were never cheeky, and the prince and princess used to look at them and say to each other:

'They are truly the best daughters in the world, even better than the English princesses were when they were little girls. It truly was the best day of our lives when we left the benighted island and came to England. Our daughters always have food to eat and water to drink and they have nice flat tummies, although Nita's tummy button does stick out a bit. But to us, they are perfect.

'We shall love them and cherish them all the rest of our days. And we will live happily ever after.'

And they did.

3

The Prodigal Daughter

The taxi turned off the dual carriageway and into the first of several tree-lined avenues. All the familiar shops were there: the travel agent, the bank, the Jewish patisserie and the baker. One shopfront was boarded up, torn fly posters fluttering, old graffiti fading. And there was a charity shop where the post office had been. Otherwise the avenue was as An remembered it.

It had been a long cold winter with frost till April. Now spring and summer seemed to butt up against each other and already it was unseasonally hot. Drought was predicted. It was early June and the cherry trees were still awash with pink and white blossoms, dropping like coloured rice paper onto the shop awnings. A good omen, thought An. Like olive branches, held aloft to welcome the prodigal. Only, the father was dead. And the family knew where she had been. Still, she had wandered in from the wilderness after a fashion. She could still make the story fit.

Summer breeze made the branches dance, then, in a sudden gust, a storm of blossom whipped around the car momentarily hiding the street from view. Instinctively, the taxi-driver switched on his windscreen wipers. They screeched across the dry glass, leaving moist ragged petals in their wake. He cursed softly under his breath. An sat forward in her seat and peered through the smeared windscreen. The street was suddenly unfamiliar. Without thinking, she rested a hand on the driver's shoulder. He threw her a glance in his rear-view mirror and caught her eye. She realised that her mouth was centimetres away from his ear. Strands of his hair, alive with the static of her proximity, tickled her left cheek. He smelled of sandalwood, Old Spice, cigarettes. Like the old man. Like Daddy. Quickly, she withdrew her hand and sat back.

'Next left please.' Her voice was louder than she had intended. The man sought her eyes in the mirror again, then manoeuvred the car down the steep hill as requested. He tilted his face so that his narrow nostrils and the thick bush of his moustache appeared briefly in the mirror. He shook his head, said something in a language she didn't understand. Laughing at her.

An leaned back into her seat, trying to look unconcerned. She stared at the big detached houses as each one emerged behind a flowering oak, searching their facades as if seeking a familiar face in the shadowed windows. The houses became progressively more ostentatious as they neared the bottom of the road. Pillars appeared under stone porches, bronze lions sprawled beside clipped hedges, smart paved driveways supporting even smarter cars, never less than two, usually three. Everyone had gone about their daily business on foot or on the buses and left their vehicles behind. Like a spare skin; a totem; beware all trespassers.

At the T-junction the taxi turned right and immediately left. Suddenly the grand houses gave way to mean little boxes, a careless lather of blues and greys and creams painted over the pebble-dash. The hedges were unkempt, the paths leading to each front door were made of crumbly uneven concrete that glowed a baleful white in the sun. But the pastel blossoms drifted here as liberally, as gaily, as anywhere else. Luxury and lack, side by side; the story of her life.

Every second of this car ride brought her nearer to the homestead. What would it be like without her twin sister, Greta? The nearest she could get to how it might feel was remembering that one year when they'd been estranged. When, at the age of sixteen, she had turned her back on her twin believing she no longer needed her. Even then Greta had still *been* there. To the rest of the family their bond may have been broken but she'd known all along it would never be that simple. The twins' relationship had gone too deep and been too subtle to be so easily dismissed. They were not much alike in nature but physically the girls were cut from the same cloth, identical as mirror images except for Greta's slick of straight thick hair. She had been a quiet, unobtrusive girl, especially when adults were around. She'd been like An's shadow for years, watching everything with a secretive smile, the witness in the wings. An knew now; she had merely been waiting her turn. Greta came into her own when the twins reached puberty, blazing a trail through the family, burning everyone with her brilliance. And her rage. And now Greta was dead. Irrevocably gone. Like Daddy.

The driver began to whistle between his teeth. It set her scalp tingling. An chafed her hands together; the dry skin rasped, counterpoint to his tuneless hissing. Making sweet music together. She felt sweat gathering in the dark creases of her palms.

Her words were a reflex; she was as startled as him. 'Stop! Stop the car. Yes, right here.' She fumbled with notes and change, dragged her suitcase and make-up bag out from under the seat and spilled onto the pavement. For a moment she swayed unsteadily in the bright light. Then she lifted her sunglasses from the chain around her neck, squinted down the road, and began to march purposefully towards Texas Street and the house of her childhood.

The taxi-driver stared at her retreating figure for a long time. He kissed his teeth and, executing a neat three-point turn, set off the way he had come.

The fence was in need of a coat of creosote, but the path shone with a fresh layer of red oxide, and a new gate hung between sun-bleached fence posts. Hydrangeas, roses, potted geraniums, peonies, straggled and shouted across the small front garden. To one side of the crazy-paved path was a small concreted area, in the centre of which stood a magnificent giant yucca. The windows glinted in the sun, the porch door stood open, heat wavered up from the ground like a glass shield around the house. The smell of dust and flowers was overwhelming.

An hesitated, suddenly faint. Gripping the handles of her luggage, she tottered forward a few feet, then stopped and leaned breathlessly against next-door-but-one's garden wall. For the first time that day she was aware of her leg aching, from the centre of her left buttock, to just below the knee. It was an old injury, and she no longer had to take the thrice daily painkillers that had kept her from screaming for the best part of a year. The physio had helped, too, and she could walk for miles again, with barely a trace of a limp. But every once in a while . . .

. . . you're reaching up for the banner again, the straps that hold it to the windows only just out of reach. You can feel the rough calico between your fingers. Although they've given it a good shake out, every time you touch it little clouds of dust puff out of the cloth and mingle with the cobwebs. They'll have to find a better place to store it. Eleven months of the year in the attic is rotting the appliqué. And a smudged hand print has transformed one letter 'T' so that the legend on the banner now takes on quite the wrong meaning. From below comes a waft of floral perfume, and a piqued voice.

'Oh look at that. The Feminist Debasing Society. We'll be the laughing stock.'

You snort, sneeze, slip. The last thing you remember is the smell of flowers, and your skirt hanging over your eyes as you swing from the ladder by one leg . . .

Her doctor says it must be psychosomatic, as the original injury is now completely healed. Get a life, he implies, find something real to worry about. But Mummy's doctor told Mummy that for years, and then had to explain to the hospital consultant why he had failed to diagnose two slipped discs. Mummy had been triumphant. Daddy, who had sided with the GP, had said, 'For a sick woman, you're as strong as an ox. Slipped disc! You'll outlive me!' And proved himself right.

An dropped her suitcase onto the pavement and gave her thigh a solid thump, like an old sergeant major. 'Game leg, don't you know. Got it fighting the Boers. Or was that the bores?'

The door opened, with a rattle and bang. The utilitarian safety glass of their childhood had been replaced with a fancy smoked affair in an abstract, swirly pattern. But the ornate metal grille protecting the glass was the same; it still didn't fit. For a while Mummy had experimented with a plastic strip curtain that later adorned the kitchen door, but it made the narrow hall look dark, and meant you couldn't see wobbly shadows of visitors coming up the path anymore. In the moment after she had rung the doorbell, An remembered how relieved she had been when the wrought iron grille had been reinstated, and the plastic curtain relegated to the back of the house. It was common. Vulgar. Made a poor first impression; she had seen her English friends giggling at it. It was just too Jamaican.

'Is Jamaican time you keeping now, eh?' Daddy's rhetorical bark startled An from her daydream. Beth's face scowled up at her, in a perfect imitation of the old man. She stepped back into the hall to let her sister pass, adding, 'Eh eh, An, is pure sweat yu sweating. D'you walk all the way from Sheffield or what?'

An limped down the hall, through the kitchen and into the dayroom. The dayroom was actually a 12' by 12' extension that housed the television and an assortment of battered arm-chairs – two orange vinyl-covered uprights and the threadbare easy chairs from the old three-piece suite that Mummy thought too good to put out for the dustmen. Potted plants wound their polished leaves around the legs. A piece of rush matting, curling dangerously at the edges, covered the centre of the orange carpet. Mummy's sewing machine, disguised in its veneered cupboard, huddled in a corner. Squeezed between the piano and the patio doors was a gingham-covered table and four chairs. An pulled out one of the chairs and flopped down, still clutching her make-up bag.

Beth deposited the suitcase at the foot of the stairs and

followed her as far as the kitchen. She took a jug from the fridge and stirred it briskly with a metal spoon, swirling up a storm of sugar. She dried glasses, then poured two generous measures of the lemonade. She added a slice of lemon and a glacé cherry on a stick to each glass. Then she took a lace doily, placed it in the centre of a wooden tray, and arranged the glasses and the jug on them. As she approached the table, An sighed and turned to face her.

'Sorry, sorry, sorry. Sorry I'm two days late and didn't get to see Mummy off. I really meant to, but I had to step in and help organise a conference at the last minute. Feminist Debating; I do it every year. I tried to explain but Mummy said to save it for you. And I'm sorry about just now. The taxi-driver was coming on to me, I had to get out. I had to walk from Stern Avenue. It's a bloody long way on a hot day with heavy bags.'

Beth sat down across the table. 'Right, that's two sorrys. You mentioned four.'

An laughed. She got up, put her arms around Beth's neck and kissed her cheek. 'No, it was only three. The last one's gratis. I'm sure we'll find a use for it later.'

Their faces were centimetres apart and they stared into each other's eyes. They rubbed their noses together, Eskimo style, and giggled. An sat down again. She raised her lemonade above her head. 'Here's looking at you, kid. It's good to be back on the ole homestead.'

'Good to have you here, pardner.' Beth took a gulp of lemonade and jumped up. 'I've got your favourite,' she called from the kitchen. 'Mincemeat and roti.'

Later, Beth remembered about the taxi-driver. 'What do you mean he was coming on to you?'

An, roti in hand, a shiny ring of sauce around her mouth, waved the question away. 'Oh, the usual, you know. Nothing I couldn't handle. Mmm, this is the best meal I've had in ages. Can I have some more mince?'

A guided tour was in order. A lot had changed in the two years since An had been at the homestead. It had started with Daddy's retirement. In fact, it seemed as if everything had started with Daddy's retirement.

'Within six month, less, it was clear he was sick. They'd talked about decorating throughout for months, and they were just waiting for Daddy to have the time, and for one of the savings policies to mature. But when it came to it, he kept putting it off and putting it off.'

Beth shut the door to the new downstairs bathroom and led the way back out to the garden. 'And you know that wasn't like him. He was always one for getting stuck in. "Never put off until tomorrow what you can do today", remember?'

An had been about to slip into one of the deckchairs that her sister was busily erecting on the lawn. The old phrase worked like a tonic. She leapt up again and began to apply herself to the garden umbrella, folded on the grass.

'Here, I'll do it,' Beth pushed her gently aside. 'Sit down. You're too cack handed. You'll have your fingers off in a snap.'

An bit her lip and did as she was told. 'So, what happened then?'

'Well, we got the decorators in, which made a nice change. They were quick, you know, and not too expensive.'

'No, I meant what happened with Daddy?'

'I bullied him into going to the doctor in the end. He wouldn't listen to Mummy. He said he wasn't old yet, just

tired, and he didn't need her showing him the grave before
he was ready. But they'd also got this cruise all planned, so I
appealed to his vanity. I said, "You're going to look pretty old
when you can't even swing your golf clubs on the deck." That
was his dream, you see. All his life. Playing golf on a cruise
ship to the Caribbean.' She gave one last flounce to the
umbrella's trim, and tilted it until the curved shadow encom-
passed both chairs.

An wanted to say, 'Golf? Cruise? Whose Daddy are we
talking about here?' The father she'd known had professed to
despise the Caribbean. It was one of his favourite rants. He'd
left there like a bat out of hell. He'd put up with all manner
of indignities in this country, including being stuck in a second
rate teaching job, just so none of his children would have to
grow up on 'those benighted islands'. And he'd never been
abroad in his whole life. Cruise? But looking across at her
sister's face, softened by the warm memories, the might-have-
beens that passed before her eyes, she said nothing.

Beth sat down, and immediately got up again. 'More
lemonade?'

'I'll get it in a minute. Finish the story.'

'I may as well, I'm up now.'

An watched her as she walked slowly back to the house
and was swallowed up by the shadowy interior. Beth had put
on a lot of weight. She was at least three dress sizes larger. In
just two years. She was beautifully dressed, as usual, in a
thigh-length silk vest and wide white cotton trousers. She still
made all her own clothes, and did her hair herself or with
their mother's help. Today she sported an African-print wrap,
at the back of which a neat cane row style could be glimpsed.
She made the most of herself, but it seemed a shame. Beth

had always been nice looking, rather than pretty, but she'd
had a stunning figure. It was a bit of a shock to see she'd let
her body go.

An thought of the presents she'd brought: a hand-stitched
silk kaftan from her own holiday in Turkey, and a pair of
stretch satin trousers she'd picked up at the Kensington
Fashion Carry at the weekend. The story about organising
a conference wasn't quite true. Rather, it was true, but the
conference had been the previous month. There was no way,
though, she could explain to Beth that she'd been in London
for four days already, staying with her friend Eloise in Brixton.

It had been nerve-racking. What if they'd bumped into each
other? Mummy had a cousin in South London, as well. What
if she'd decided to visit her before going away? They might
have taken a jaunt over to the market, come face to face over
some best okra and yellow yam. Eloise had had to remind her
that Mummy and the aunt, Mummy's cousin, were going
away together, and neither of them would be buying pro-
visions. They might have needed some extra cases though.
Mummy was always buying suitcases. What she did with
them, only she knew. But Eloise asssured her that even
Mummy wouldn't be out buying suitcases three days before
taking a trip of a lifetime. She'd probably packed weeks ago.
Still it had been a tense time.

An did feel guilty about it. She knew Mummy and Beth
would be disappointed. Mummy would hide it beneath a ven-
eer of scorn. She could almost hear her, venting her anger at
Beth. 'That girl. Well, what do you expect? Your sister
"couldn't make it" when they told us about your Dad's heart.
She "couldn't make it" when he went into hospital, or when
he came out to die. An "couldn't make it" to the funeral.

What makes you think she'll "make it" now? I'm only going
on a three-month cruise with your Aunty Vi. That's nothing
to write home about.'

Would Beth have defended her? Or had An let her down
once too many times as well? She sat up in her chair as Beth
emerged from the house, carrying a tray laden with drinks
and ice-cream. The clothes wouldn't fit, of course. She
couldn't even show them to her, it would only remind Beth
of how big she'd got. So it would look like she'd stayed away
for two years and not even brought her sister a present. A
no-win situation.

The sun was directly overhead and getting hotter. The
umbrella had been moved half a dozen times, and each time
the bright blazing day had crept around again and knocked
the shadow away. Now a small black circle, the exact circum-
ference of the garden table, was all that was left. Wasps buzzed
over the remains of the ice-cream. An assortment of green
and black flies floated in the lemonade.

An's head tilted back over the top of her deckchair and her
mouth had started to droop. Beth came back from washing
the dishes to find her sister snoring gently. Beads of sweat
had popped up on her forehead, and began to trickle into her
ears. Beth gathered up the debris on the table, trying not to
clink the glasses. As she reached for the jug, a wasp rose
angrily from under the rim and zipped past her face. With a
muffled cry, she drew back, her eyes swivelling to see where
it had gone. The jug toppled onto the lawn without a sound.

'Oh damn.' She bent to pick it up. The handle came away
in her hand, leaving two neat bowls of glass rocking in the
grass. 'Damn, double damn.'

Beth sat back on her haunches, and dangled the handle from one finger. She looked down the long garden towards the house. At the patio her father had laid three years ago, with its neat concrete wall. At the hanging baskets and potted plants now wilting in the heat despite twice-daily watering. At the sticks for the runner beans they didn't plant this year; the rose bushes, tied up in preparation for creosoting the fence; and the fence itself, pale brown and splintering, neglected. Despite this, the house was one of the smartest on the street. The windows always gleamed. The paths were always swept, the pebble-dash touched up and the red brick repainted every year. This year was no exception. Only, once they'd finished refitting the downstairs rooms they had had to postpone some of the more fiddly jobs. Not just because Daddy had been too sick to do the work, or because she and Mummy had been so busy. After Daddy came out of hospital that last time, Mummy had wanted nothing at all to disturb his peace. No smells, or sounds, and, as far as possible, no reminders of what he could no longer do.

He had been a long time dying, the old man. He'd wilted and curled up like the flowers. He'd faded and splintered and come apart until he was someone she didn't know at all. And everything that had gone before seemed meaningless in the face of such a death. Because after it there could be nothing else. No redemption. No renewal. No swinging golf clubs on the deck after all the years of hard work, the years of suffering.

That was why she'd insisted her mother use the cruise tickets. It had taken some organising, to change the itinerary and get Aunt Vi's name on the documentation in place of her father's. But in the end it had worked out perfectly. There'd

been time for the funeral and sorting out the essential administration immediately after the death. Time to breathe again
before preparing for the holiday.

There'd even been time for a family reunion with An but
that hadn't happened. She'd been too busy with her studies,
she'd claimed. She had to work hard if she was to catch up
with her group after her year out. Keep her nose to the grind-
stone. Apply herself diligently. Daddy phrases, well chosen;
for how could Mummy and Beth argue against the old man's
words? And now here she was, snoring peacefully in the sun
as if she'd never been away.

It is always summer and the song of the ice cream van tinkles
down the wide streets. Leaves dapple yellow and green, fil-
tering shadows, and the air is as light as sea breezes. They
come in distant waves; laughter, the joyful screams of children,
chanted rhymes. You can almost smell the salt, a displaced
memory from another time, the clatter of the train to Hastings
making the pavement shiver. A ball bounces, ticking down
the tarmac, metronome of all your days; time passes, slow and
sweet and steady. Run, jump, skip, fly, there is nothing you
can't do. The threads of life weave from your fingertips like
rainbow coloured streamers. You are spinning a world, light
as a web, casting your net in a shimmering circle. See it vault
and hold, see it catch in the branches, let it snare, there, a
gossamer temple in the tree tops for you to find and shelter
in whenever you close your eyes.

Here are the things you do: walk the top of the red brick
wall and jump; aeroplane over the playing fields; hold hands
in a human chain and squeal through the cobwebs at the back
of the shed; kiss the best-looking-boy-in-the-whole-school;

win at marbles; win at jacks. You are all things bright and beautiful. Your smile is a thin bright line, stretched as far as it will go – and it goes far, much further than you think it could, getting thinner and brighter all the time – a spider's silk that you stride across. In your spangles and dancing shoes, in your head held high, with a flick of the wrist and a turn of the screw . . .

Here are the things that are hidden: trading sniffs and musky tastes in the toilets at break time; rifling through crowds of empty coats during assembly; cheating in tests; stealing sweets from the corner shop; playing knock-down-ginger through the flats; fighting. Small crimes all, but crimes all the same. Signs and symbols, shadows of the iceberg. Indications.

He chants over you, like praying but not to your God. He is the one true God, with his all-seeing eye, his masks and his revenges. Repeat after him: you are a bad girl and you must be punished. You are a bad girl and you must be punished, you are a bad bad bad bad girl. And you must be punished.

4

Welcome to the Ole Homestead

An stood on the threshold and waited for the pain to subside. She'd woken with one hell of a headache. It wasn't until her dazzled eyes met the gloom inside the extension that it really hit. It felt as if a mallet was pounding away on top of her head. The shock waves reverberated through her and she began to tremble uncontrollably. Swallowing hard, she put a hand on either side of the door frame to steady herself. After a couple of minutes the pounding became a dull thump and she was able to walk.

The venetian blinds were closed and the room was silent and cool. An's nose began to run with the sudden change in temperature. Sniffing, arms folded tight over her chest, she made her way slowly through the downstairs rooms.

On closer inspection, the changes to the house were less drastic than they had appeared. The kitchen was the same as before, except for the addition of some new appliances and a scatter of spotlights in the ceiling. The through-lounge, that seemed to have taken on cathedral-like proportions when she'd first peered around the door, had merely been skilfully decorated in a variety of pale tones. The same embossed wallpaper her mother favoured, but now in ivory instead of light green. And the Carpetworld best patterned Axminster had given way to a beige Berber with subtle flecks of grey and brown. The gold dralon sofa was the same, but the linen antimacassars (hand stitched by Mummy as a girl) had gone.

An detected her sister's hand. Mummy liked detail, lots of it, floral prints, rich fabrics and colours, ornamental clutter. Beth, with her eye for simplicity and order, had not managed to dispense with all the fripperies – the glass animals still paraded across the mantelpiece; the sugar starch orange doily in the shape of a swan kept pride-of-place on the coffee table. But somehow a compromise had been reached. Mummy's bits and pieces looked folksy, ethnic, in their spacious new setting.

An walked under the wide arch and into the dining-room area. Being at the back of the house, the room did not attract much natural light. The building of the dayroom hadn't helped. Now Mummy had added a cream-coloured net curtain, dense with embroidery, to the French windows between this room and the extension. The oval banqueting table gleamed quietly in the shadowed room. An slid her fingers over the glossy surface, remembering it decked out for Christmas and Easter. Cut glass ware, Royal Doulton dinner service, silver plated cutlery, linen napkins in silver filigree rings. The heavy candelabra matched the cutlery, and there were extra sets of both.

'For you girls when you grow up,' Mummy used to say. 'For when you set up house with your husbands.'

She showed them how to remove the dull gold tarnish from the silverware and restore each tiny section with a soft cloth and a pot of silver polish. There would be generations of Moores, albeit under other as yet unknown names, sitting at tables groaning with glistening opulence. Mummy made immortal through her choice of tableware.

Squeezing past the upholstered carver chair, An approached the sideboard. Mummy had bought a new, ceiling height display unit with matching drinks cabinet some years ago but the sideboard, a near flawless survivor from the 1960s, had never been replaced, merely complemented. Squatting, An opened it now and surveyed the contents. All the old favourites were there, from a time when lack of money had necessitated a simpler style: two brown and dark yellow dinner services, that could be mixed and matched; an array of plain wine glasses; four stainless steel goblets, one for each member of the family, with their names etched on the surface in a design of flowers.

There was a soft, fragrant smell. An put her hand in the cupboard, gently moving things aside. At the back she found a box of ancient sugared jellies set out, yellow and orange, in an overlapping wheel. An unpicked the Sellotape and prised off the plastic lid. She selected the red sweet at the centre of the wheel. It was fat and plump as a jellyfish, and smelled of flowers. After she sucked off the crust, it disintegrated in her mouth in a sickly trickle.

An got to her feet. Something in the corner of the room, on top of the sideboard, caught her eye. She reached into the shadows and touched cold metal. It was the peanut tin. Yellow, white and blue with a photo on the front of a striped bowl piled high with peanuts, looking luscious and crisp. When they were very small Daddy used to take them down to Woolworth's on the Broadway, every Saturday. They could have a quarter of pick-and-mix each, and he'd get a pound of nuts to refill the tin. He didn't keep the nuts all to himself, he shared them out. With parsimonious exactitude he would dole nuts into their waiting palms, staring at each one as it fell as if it was a tiny gold nugget. He used a light, sprinkling movement. If he was too free with his wrist action and a sudden shower of nuts descended, the fingers of his free hand would fly out and decimate the pile, leaving no more than was proper for a small child to consume.

'Ai-oh,' he'd grunt, 'that's enough.'

It was a joke, of sorts. Peanuts were Daddy's only savoury treat. He had a confirmed sweet tooth. Mummy continually warned him against diabetes – The Sugar. 'We're not Back Home now, y'know. You can't sweat it all out in this cold climate. Sugar, salt, spice, it's not good for you; you'll overload your heart.'

As she turned to leave the room, An wondered where the toddler-size china Pekinese dogs had got to. For years they had dominated the window recess, keeping guard over the giant rubber plant. An shuddered at the memory, 'An ugly pair of pests if ever I saw them. Too, too Jamaican by half.'

'Who is?' Beth pushed open the door just as An reached for the handle.

'Jeez, Beth, you scared the life out of me.'

'I was out front, watering the flowers. I thought I saw you moving about in here.' She shifted the watering can into her left hand and rubbed the shine off her nose with her right. She glanced around the room as if checking that everything was in place, then went into the kitchen to put the can under the sink. An hovered in the doorway.

'Do you like it?'

'The room? Yes. Very tasteful. The old girl must really have been glad to have you home; she's let you run riot with the family purse.'

Beth carried on washing her hands. Her lips moved as she whispered under her breath: 'seven, eight, nine, ten.' She dried her hands and hung the towel back on its hook. Leaning against the worksurface, she folded her arms and smiled. 'So, what do you want to do now?'

'I've got a bitch of a headache, to be honest. I could do with a lie-down.'

At the top of the stairs, An turned right. She paused outside her parents' bedroom. Mummy's room. The door was closed. Had Mummy and Beth rearranged the past in there also? Had they thrown away the velvet curtains and put up bamboo blinds? Painted the walls white and stripped the floorboards? Burned the old mattress and hung bunting from the fitted wardrobes? She pressed her hand against the avocado gloss paint. No. Not yet. Turning, she opened instead the door immediately in front of her.

The boxroom was untouched. As she went in a gust of air lifted the nets. An saw the high wall where once a terrace of houses had stood, and through the open window heard the muffled drone of the motorway. It was always a shock. They must have extended the M1 ten, fifteen years ago, yet she could never get used to seeing a blank expanse of dusty concrete instead of the homes of her first playmates.

An squeezed around the door and sat down on the bed. This room was as tiny as ever. No amount of interior decorator's tricks could have improved its dimensions. There was barely enough space for the single bed, chest of drawers, and a rushwork stool that served as a bedside table. It had a spartan simplicity to it, and despite the best efforts of the eight-lane highway not three hundred yards away, a peace that she had always loved.

Here she had read the letters of Van Gogh to his brother, identifying with all his agony, seeing her little stool as a symbol of affinity, representative of his own bedroom chair. She'd followed up with the Russians: *The Brothers Karamazov, War and Peace* and the works of Dostoevsky. She had revised for her A level resits, sprawled on this very bed. And before that, had sat on the floor under the window, dreaming about her boyfriend in preference to cramming for her exams. Her books still sat in the bed-head that Daddy had made: white melamine and padded vinyl, with a little recessed shelf and a reading light. Here stood her fledgling collection of pill boxes, all five of them, and the corn-dolly in bonnet and cape she'd bought on a school trip.

'Er, An? Are you awake?' Beth shuffled nervously outside on the landing. After a moment, she put her head around the door. 'Hi.'

'Hi. I was just saying hello to my room.'

'I'm sorry, I should have told you before.' Beth pushed open the door as far as it would go and inched her way in. She had a pained look on her face.

'What? What's the matter?'

'Well, you see, I'm in here now.'

An looked around the room, not understanding – of course Beth was in there; she'd just opened the door and come in. Then she caught sight of a dressing gown, hanging on a hook behind the door. She hadn't noticed it before. Perhaps because it was the same colour as the one she used to have as a child, peach and white. Except that had been thrown out years ago, and was made of humble brushed cotton. This was made of thick smooth satin, trimmed on the collar and cuffs with a wide strip of peach ribbon. More luxurious than anything she'd ever owned. More like something Mummy might buy (in the sales, of course). Only it was Beth's, and looked as if she had bought it yesterday.

An stood up quickly. 'Oh, no, it's my fault, I shouldn't have expected . . . I assumed.'

They hesitated at the door, then Beth picked up her sister's make up bag and backed out of the room. It was awkward, both of them trying to get out at the same time. Beth was saying, 'I was in the other room, but I moved in here a few weeks before Daddy died. Mummy wanted me near them, so I could hear if she needed help.' An was saying, 'That's fine, really. The back bedroom's just as good. I need the wardrobe anyway.'

Then somehow they were pressed together just outside the room. Near enough for an Eskimo kiss. Their eyes met.

An reached out without looking for her bag. 'Thanks. Thanks, I'll be fine now.' She backed into the other room and shut the door. After a while, Beth's footsteps receded down the stairs.

An leaned against the cool gloss-painted door. This room, overlooking the garden, only got the sun in the middle of the day. It was now late afternoon and a light breeze lifted the homemade austrian blinds and dropped them again. She looked at the twin beds with their matching homemade bed-heads and Pierrot quilt covers. The melamine bookcase, full of nursery books: *My First Illustrated Dictionary; A Child's Garden of Verse; The Fairy Tales of Hans Christian Andersen*. Beth had dusted and hoovered and put a vast bowl of fresh flowers on top of the dressing table. Her suitcases were balanced on top of the wardrobe, two of her outfits hung over the side in clear plastic zip-covers. But essentially, the room remained the same, a testament to Mummy's and Daddy's creative urges. An released a long breath. She let a single tear slide down each cheek. She had thought she'd never have to sleep in this room again.

'Hello, room,' she said tentatively. The room said nothing at all.

There was nothing else to do, she may as well start the dinner. It didn't seem right to sit in the garden, enjoying the last of the sunshine, with An upstairs, upset.

An was right, though she probably hadn't meant it: she would be better off in the back bedroom. It was more spacious, and judging from the amount of make-up on An's face, she would appreciate the dressing table with its bevelled edge mirror. The matching wardrobe creaked and clacked with the music of empty hangers; An could put all her designer clothes away. Her tart's trousseau of basques and batty riders, and all those figure-hugging little lycra numbers. No doubt she would say they were her way of making the personal political – whatever we wear, wherever we go, yes means yes and no means no. No wonder men were always 'coming on to her', and, as usual, An wanted it both ways. Yeah, the back bedroom would suit An just fine. There was even a choice of beds for when she was in two minds. Schizoid.

Beth reached into the fridge and pulled out the chicken. She ripped open the butcher's thin white plastic bags and began to wash the bird in a stream of cold water. After a brief rinse, she got a metal bowl from the cupboard under the sink, poured in some vinegar and more water, and began to give the chicken a thorough bath.

She was meticulous, as Mummy had taught her to be. 'Can't stand the way English people buy meat and throw it straight in the pan. No washing, nothing. It coulder dropped on the floor, someone sneezed on it. You never know where it's been. You ever looked at a butcher's apron? And you want us to eat in restaurant, restaurant all the time? Huh, mmn. No sir. I don't trust these people at all, at all.' It was a wonder she wasn't vegetarian. But then, soil had all kinds of faeces raked into it, and people walking on it with their dirty boots. May as well eat meat, just so long as it's clean.

Back and front, under each wing, pull out the legs and rub inside the creases. Open the neck; draw up the parson's nose, wash out each cavern. Pluck any remaining hairs between index finger and the back of a knife. Pat dry and rub all over with half a lemon, before finishing up with a dusting of salt, outside and in. It was like bathing a baby. A tiny dead baby. Tenderly, Beth laid the bird on the wooden chopping block and paused, her palms on the cool dome of its breast.

At the back of the counter, secured to the tiled wall, stood the knife rack. Instinctively, Beth reached for the chopper. She kissed her teeth as her fingers met air. She could never remember. They'd put the knives away, of course – years ago, when An was reaching her peak, just before she went away – in the only drawer in the kitchen with a lock. Well that was over and done now. Beth opened the drawer with a yank, found a chopper amongst the tangle of utensils, and began to dismember the chicken with swift savage blows. As soon as she was finished, she'd find every last blasted knife and put it right back. Let An see them. Let her dare. Beth was ready for her any time.

*   *   *

That was how she'd put on so much weight; always cooking. 'Proper food', like Mummy had taught her: stew chicken, baked chicken, jerk chicken; patties, curries, souse and cowfoot; red beans, gunga peas, split peas and black-eyes, with or without rice, but always with a little something – garlic and chopped onion, a sprig of thyme or a chunk of pig fat. Soups heaving with knuckle bones, dumplings bobbing on the top – the soft white variety, or the heavy cornmeal dumplings that keeled over at the touch of a spoon and nosedived to the bottom of the bowl – bitter-sweet drinks like sorrel, Guinness punch, lemonade. Then there was the baking – the coconut cakes and banana breads, bun just like grandma used to make: at Christmas the densest, richest, rummiest black cake, groaning under an inch of marzipan and a crust of royal icing. Equally, she liked English food, Mummy had taught her that too. Roast dinners, pies, lashings of gravy; the hot-breathed puff of a perfect Yorkshire pudding, at that moment when you first plunge your knife in; the tart sweetness of lemon meringue pie. Most recently she had discovered nouvelle cuisine. Delightful deli raids, Greek grocers and the fruits of Harrods food hall; all of it worked like a sedative. Cooking calmed her, the process of it, the vigour and the gentleness. Like when she was making meringues and she had to beat the eggs, then fold in the sugar. Beat and fold, enfold, cherish. Beth wiped her hands and breathed in the smells coming from the pots now simmering on the cooker.

Poor An, her ears must have been burning her. Of course she was upset. It was understandable. She'd always loved that little boxroom, had been ecstatic when Mummy agreed she could move into it when she was sixteen. And the back room surely held memories An would not wish to revisit. But Beth was settled now, and after all, she was the one who lived in the house. Her comfort was at least as important as An's, who was merely passing through, who could no longer call this house home. This was probably the best way, anyway. An couldn't be coddled for ever. At some point in her life, she had to stand on her own two feet. Face up to the truth and put the past behind her. Now was as good a time as any.

Having governed her temper and the dinner, Beth felt satisfied. She opened the drawer again and sifted through the contents until she had retrieved all the knives. One by one she slotted them into their little grooves, in order of size, with the paring knife on the left and the chopper on the right. Of course, it was nonsense about the knives. It always had been. Mummy and Daddy overreacting, getting carried away with the drama of the situation. Beth ran her finger lightly along the blade of the chopper. It was a little dull. She'd really had to whack that chicken apart, even if she hadn't been in a strop. Still, she'd wait a while, till the end of the summer when An was gone, before she sharpened it.

5

The Twins

Two girls, one bright one dark, navigate the early years with billowing sails. Two small girls, not quite but sisters, best of friends for ever amen. If you cry, so do I. If you die, so will I. Promise you, cross your heart.

Up the road and round the corner, over the back and over the playing fields. In her yard and in your garden, whispering secrets, telling tales. In the playground, in the classroom, at assembly, after school's out. Weekends, weekdays, church and Sunday school, spinning stories, spinning tales.

Your mum, her mum going shopping; down the Broadway, up the Central. Cross the Boroughs to the library, trading stories, tickets for tales. If the teacher sees you, hide it. Just tell Miss that you can't find it, learn to keep it safe and buried or they'll say you're telling tales.

Two girls, one dark one darker, like twin shadows, each seeking shelter; 'home' is only one another, whispering secrets, telling tales. Don't let go of her, she'll never leave you, always ready to relieve you, stepping in when you can't take it, when your back's against the rails.

That's what twins are for.

At school, from infants to age eight, it was Anita and her best friend Daphne. Nita and Nep. An and Dap. Dap was as 'fair' as An was dark, her hair as soft as An's was tight. Later, An was as secretive as Dap was open. No-one could see what they had in common.

An used to wish they really were sisters. She used to pray about it, thinking if she was really good for a whole week she'd wake up one morning and Dap's Mum would be her Mum. Dap's big sister would be her big sister. Dap's Dad, who was hardly ever there because he was with some fancy woman or other, would be her Dad who was hardly ever there . . . But God had other ideas. When they were eight Dap was moved into another class across the hall. It might as well have been another school. The teachers said it was for the best. The girls would concentrate better if they were separated.

It wasn't that An didn't love her own family. Only that things were . . . difficult. At home. That's what her teacher, Miss Thomas, used to say. Usually after An had been caught stealing or fighting or snogging boys or committing one of a dozen other misdemeanours that at first seemed so out of character, but were rapidly becoming just what you'd expect of Anita Moore. Miss Thomas was small and mousy and kind. She kept faith with An, the real An. She kept her back after the bell rang. An would sit, eyes sliding from Miss Thomas's face, watching the children scream around the playground. Miss Thomas would hold her hand. Sometimes she'd cup her finger under An's chin trying to get her to look at her. An didn't mind. It was nice; the attention, the fuggy classroom smelling of hot paint and damp children. Their little talks were circular – Miss Thomas never really expected any answers to her questions. They usually ended with Miss Thomas sighing and saying, 'I suppose things are . . . difficult. At home.'

Miss Tart was not so kind. She expected proper answers to all her questions and Anita had better not be so cheeky as to look her in the eye. One day, An stood in the headmistress's office with her hands clasped at her front. Miss Tart gestured to a little pile of coppers on her desk.

'This is the third time this week. This was found in your plimsoll bag after several children complained of lunch money going missing. Do you have any explanation at all?'

'No, Miss.'

'Are you saying you *didn't* steal this money?'

'No, Miss.'

'Well, that's good at least. I can't tolerate a liar as well as a thief. I'm waiting, Anita.'

'Yes, Miss.'

'Well?'

'What, Miss?'

'Miss Tart, Anita. "What, Miss Tart".'

At Anita's puzzled stare, Miss Tart stood up then quickly sat down again. She was getting frustrated now. She drummed her fingernails on the desk. The coins tinkled and slid across its surface.

'Why are you stealing?' she said, slowly and carefully.

'My sister told me to, Miss.'

'Sister? Nonsense, I don't believe it. Lisa-Beth was a model pupil, we never had a moment's worry with Lisa. Anyway, your sister went up to comprehensive last year. It will be your turn soon and I can tell you this, Anita, they won't stand for this kind of behaviour there. Not at all.'

'My twin sister, Miss. Not Beth, Greta. Greta told me to. It's only pennies, we never take real money.'

'This is real money. This is stealing.' She leapt up again and began to circle the child and the desk. An watched her triangular buttocks jiggle in their beige high-waister slacks. As the head mistress completed her circuit her tweedle-dee tummy came into view, high and round and menacing. She was funny, with her odd shape and her 'al all' instead of at all. An smiled.

'I'm at a loss to understand it, really I am,' said Miss Tart, more to herself than to An. 'You come from a perfectly good family. Goodness, your Daddy's a teacher. What would he have to say about all this, mmm? mmmm?'

Suddenly she turned on An, furious and confused, white in the face. An stepped back, blinking. 'Wipe that grin off your face! I want to hear no more about it. No more stealing, no more meddling with the boys, no more fighting. And Anita, I won't tolerate a liar. Now get back to your class at once.'

And that was the end of that.

Walking back from her Saturday job, Beth passes his house. She passes it a dozen times a week and she never looks to see if he's there. She doesn't have to. She can feel his presence from across the street. At first he only stood in his bedroom window, gazing forlornly at the pavement below. From the corner of her eye she'd see the curtain drop and know that his mother had walked into the room. He'd get a beating for that; mooning out of the window like a fool for all the neighbours to see. Beth, walking home with her bags, lets the tears fall, silent and unhindered.

After a time he stands outside the front door. Mrs Goode has beaten him beyond fear by now, there's nothing more she can do to him. He holds his head up, waiting sentry, and follows Beth along the street with his eyes.

Today he crosses the street and tries to take her bags from her. She resists and, since he won't fight her, he falls back and lets her go on her way. Then he changes his mind.

'They can call me names and beat me. They can kill me if they like. But it's not over, Betty. It's only over if you say you don't love me.'

It sounds like a speech from a film. They would have laughed about that. Before. Beth watches her feet, marching up Texas Street. Her mouth feels like it's stuck fast. There is absolutely nothing she can say that is worth saying anymore. He dogs her like a shadow.

'Betty, please. Please, Betty.'

They get nearer and nearer to her house. They both know he doesn't have much time, and that this will be the last time. Desperation wails in his voice.

'You've given up, haven't you?' He stands in front of her and blocks her way. 'I can't believe you'd do this to us. There's nothing they could do to me that would make me treat you so cold.'

He sounds very young, petulant and outraged. Beth knows she is very, very old. A century of experience separates them. She adjusts the weight of her shopping bags and steps around him.

'Go home, George,' she says. 'It's over.'

6

Games Children Play

The sewing machine was a wedding present. Not, it transpired, from a wedding guest, a wealthy family member or a life-long friend; the 'girls' – the other nurses – hadn't clubbed together to give her a gift worthy of a new bride; her husband hadn't wandered the length of Tottenham Court Road, teetering on the brink outside Heal's, mulling it over outside Maple's before plunging in and buying her every housewife's dream.

It came from Mrs Moore, with love to Mrs Moore; she had bought it herself. Not outright, of course. She'd put a bit down every month, peeling the worn notes off her meagre pay packet and pressing them into the eager palm of the sales assistant. Two long-kept, awful, exhilarating secrets: the sewing machine and the size of her pay-packet. Bernard didn't approve of the never-never. 'If you can't cover it, don't covet it', was his constant refrain during the early years. She suspected him of making that one up. It was a calculated risk; he'd hit the roof if he found out and he would find out, the day the delivery van unloaded her prize onto the pavement and the men wheeled it up the path and over the threshold like a museum piece, under the curious eyes of the neighbours.

It was worth it. The extra heartbeats, every drop of sweat, the beating. The day she unpacked that sewing machine was the day she felt herself to be a woman. She had arrived.

It sat in its own cabinet of grained, stained wood, wide dark stripes alternating with thin pale strips. The edges were smoothed off, rounded. Perfect for protecting children from nasty knocks. The varnish was so thick you'd have to take a chisel to it before you caused it damage. It shone secretive in its corner, pretending to be a cupboard instead of the means of her liberation, the medium of her creativity. It was truly beautiful.

The lid, made of one solid sheet of polished wood, lifted off to the left to make a little table supported by the open cabinet door underneath. Then you pulled a handle here, twiddled a something there – flick! – and the sewing machine sat proud. Underneath was the treadle wheel and the wiring for conversion to electricity. The electric treadle was a black plastic lozenge, grooved and slick as a slab of liquorice. It harboured springs and a secret power she quickly learned to ride. Evening after evening, long into the night sometimes, rushing and whoahing down seams of sheeting like a rodeo cowboy.

Frocks followed, then trouser suits, summer blazers, shirts. The children complained of lumpy gussets, plucking at themselves delicately between the legs, pulling at the wadded fabric. Buttons would not fit button-holes; they either wedged behind them refusing to shift, or slipped their moorings at the slightest breath. She learned to make do, to patch up and adjust, to unpick and restitch. After two weeks of sewing, before someone else's wedding, the bright image of her imagination – her daughters, hand in hand, in perfect party gowns – slipped, and revealed two slipshod sorry-for-themselves small girls, whining, 'Oh, Mummy, *must* we.'

Finally, she conceded defeat. She kept her hand in, though, periodically producing curtains and cushions that never quite sat straight and came unexpectedly unravelled. Still, it was a comfort to know that Beth had taken her love of cloth, colour, texture, and made it into something loveable.

Beth smoothed her hand over the patterned fabric. Great blowzy blooms in orange and green against a cream background. It was a daring choice; she usually stuck to plain colours or simple geometrics. But she felt like being different this summer. Maybe it was the near tropical heat, the lazy sultriness of the days. She pictured herself shimmering in the summer light, a tall drink in one hand, a handsome fellow on the other, looking full-blown and gorgeous in calf-length chintz with shoe-string shoulder straps. Why not? Everyone else flirted with love. Sometimes it seemed as if the whole world was made up of couples. She was young yet; why should she alone be celibate? She slid the last half dozen pins from the careful grip of her clamped mouth. Just one more seam to go, then the trimming and finishing and a tiny mother-of-pearl button to close the neckline at the back.

But she'd done enough for now. It had been a long day. Beth stood and began to pack up. She felt like a magician when she did this, closing down her box of tricks with a final flourish. There was something very satisfying about working on Mummy's machine. She hadn't bothered to use her own since she'd come home. Hers was top of the range, state of the art, up to the minute, but it didn't have history. It didn't have soul.

A desultory flick through the TV listings confirmed that there was nothing worth watching on telly. An had gone to bed early, in pursuit of beauty sleep. She'd complained of a headache again, after dinner. Perhaps it was true. An certainly looked tired and a little tense. Beth wondered, briefly, if she was on any medication. She didn't like to ask.

She curled up in one of the saggy armchairs with the remote control and a bowl of chocolate raisins. It was a toss-up between a seventies spy thriller with a risible plot that she'd seen at least twice before and a comedy chat show that didn't make her laugh. Beth stared at the screen, swapping between the two channels, trying not to think. When the chat show was replaced by *The News Tonight* she gave up and went upstairs to bed.

On her way back from the bathroom she paused outside the back bedroom. She could hear moaning, the thump and creak of An tossing in her sleep. Beth opened the door as quietly as she could and peered in. The blinds were down but both reading lights had been left on. The room glowed quietly, blurring the shadows in the corners. An had thrown the quilt and top sheet onto the floor and lay naked on one of the beds, an arm covering her eyes. In the soft light, her skin was an inky smudge against the pale pink bed-linen.

Suddenly An shivered, half sat up, then twisted herself into a clenched, foetal position. Without meaning to, Beth stepped back into the passageway out of sight. Then she heard An sobbing, helplessly, hopelessly, like a small child who has been lost for a long time and has given up believing that Mummy will come for her.

Beth tiptoed over to the bed. 'An? An-bo.'

An snuffled and stopped crying. Was she awake? Was she

listening? A memory came, unbidden, into Beth's mind. An as Tutankhamun, hands crossed over her chest, serene and smiling. On this same bed, in just a nylon nightie. Waiting for the Killing Game to start. She'd always shivered with excitement as Beth slipped the tights around her neck. Would she thrill to feel it now? Offer herself up, holding on, holding in the terror, the scream, the signal to stop, till the last possible moment?

Beth reached out to touch her, changed her mind and reached instead for the sheet on the floor. She pulled it gently over her sister's angular form, noting the sharpness of her hip bones, the arms as thin and lacking in muscle as a child's. As she folded back the pink cotton, An jutted out her chin and raised a blank, blind face towards her. A deep frown appeared between her eyebrows. Her mouth opened a fraction and she groaned.

'An-bo,' Beth said again. 'It's alright, I'm right here.'

She waited beside the bed for a long moment, perhaps a minute, perhaps thirty, until she felt herself beginning to nod and rock on her heels. Time to turn in. Beth tiptoed back to the door and stepped onto the brightly lit landing. As she pulled the door shut she heard An's breathing, low and even.

The garden stretches into the distance, apple- and pear-treed, pathed and lawned and vast. Mummy's hands at the small of your back nudge you on.

'I'm just going down the Broadway to fetch a few things. I'll be back in half an hour.' Turns and clicks lady heel back towards the house. Stops at the kitchen door.

'Lisa-Beth, you're in charge. Anita, none of your carry on;

min' your sister, you hear me?' Frown and disapproving lips move into the shadows. Shuts and locks the door and she's gone.

Beth starts. 'I'm the king, right, and I've got this band of trusty men and true. And we go over here, yeah, marching, like this, to repel the snurgents. The snurgents at the border. You're the enemy. You've got to stand there. I'm coming round the apple tree 'cos that's the border, yeah, and I lead my men in a charge against you. No, you've got to stand still, you're the enemy. Charge, men, chaaaarge!'

You come off worst. You always do. Ages later the Light Brigade have massacred all the Zulus. The Germans have suffered a crushing defeat at the hands of the Allies. A hundred elephants have carried Tarzan through the jungle and trampled the savages.

Finally you drag yourself out from under Beth. 'Got a brilliant idea.'

'You're dead, you're not supposed to move.'

'Let's storm the house. Climb the flying buttresses and breach their defences.'

A brilliant idea. You can't find the flying buttresses, so an upturned bucket will have to do. Beth's ten, the eldest; she gets to do the breaching, you hold the bucket. The hopper window over the french doors is ajar, a finger's stretch away. Nearly, nearly. You crouch on the ground. Beth is like a ballerina, reaching high above your head.

Another idea takes you. What if . . . ? Greta whispers in your ear, 'Pull it, then. Then she'll dance for you on the tips of her toes.'

You snicker, Beth looks down, Greta knocks the bucket from under her. There's a sound. A squishy thunking sound like when Daddy's chopping pig's trotters for souse. Blood pours into Beth's eyes.

7

The Circus Is Coming

Poor Pierrot, so pale and sad. He sits on the bed on a curving moon, hat in the stars, eyes cast down. Always a single tear, falling for the things he has seen and can never say. A child was born on this bed. Another died on this bed. He held them both in his full-sleeved arms and wept for them. His mouth is very small. He rests a heavy head in one hand. And will not tell.

As soon as she woke, An raised the Austrian blinds and tied loose knots in the net curtains, revealing the view from the open window. Outside the sun was already high, making everything seem flat and precise. She leaned forward and drew several deep breaths. Here in the shadow of the house the air was still cool. She stretched her hands out of the window and watched the goose bumps push up on them. Her skin was ashen, dry patches streaking up her arms. She needed some TLC. A good brush down and a soak in lavender water.

An had slept badly, as she'd known she would. Her dreams had been psychedelic; snatches of colour and sound, grotesque faces, the sensation of her heart pounding so hard in her chest she could feel the reverberations. She had had a long, involved dream about an island that had started like the one in *The Swiss Family Robinson* and ended like *Lord of the Flies*. Interspersed with this were moments, no, whole tracts of time, of pure blackness, pressing down over her body. She might have been awake, she wasn't sure. But there was something intensely familiar about this 'black sleep', something that had terrified yet intrigued her. An distinctly remembered trying to stay with it, to explore this thing that had her swelling up to fill the corners of the room, then shrinking inside until she was nothing but a tiny bone, a piece of gristle in the spongy mass of her own body. But she'd had to pull back from it. Too deep. Without her therapist on hand, An didn't dare take that journey. Several times she'd woken up drenched in sweat and shivering, and had been lulled back to sleep by the noisy silence of the suburban night. It was a relief to open her eyes to morning.

From her perch on the bed she could see the backs of the red-roofed council houses that she'd passed yesterday in the taxi. At this angle they were uniform, functional, fanning out in a neat semi-circular terrace. They glittered in the morning sun like a child's toy set. Someone had strung multi-coloured bunting between two upstairs windows and it fluttered in a festive smile with every breeze.

Without knocking, Beth pushed open the door and peered into the room. 'Oh, I didn't think you'd be up yet. It's nine o'clock. I've brought some tea.'

An reached under her pillow for a T-shirt, and slipped it over her head.

'What were you doing?'

'Air bathing. It's really good for the skin. Refreshing. We

cover ourselves up too much in this country. The skin needs to breathe.' She looked critically at Beth's dressing gown.

'I don't think so.' Beth sat down on the bed and handed An a cup. She took a sip from her own and gave a satisfied sigh. 'As soon as the sun shines here the natives put their bits out. Pink or pasty. Uuugh! If it ain't pretty, put it away, I say.' She shrugged and tossed her hair, pulling the peach satin closed over her chest.

They sat in silence for a minute, drinking and staring out of the window.

'It's funny,' An said at last, 'I was thinking about bunting just yesterday. Remember that circus by the Welsh Harp? And we all went, at night, way past our bedtime. Maybe it was only eight o'clock or something, but it felt really late, with the dark and all the lights and fairground music. Magic. I'll never forget. And the pantomime every year. They used to do that thing where all the kids had to stamp their feet and scream as loud as they could? We used to go crazy. And afterwards you could go up and help yourself to sweets or chocolates or whatever else was going free. I'm still regretting the time we went to see *Treasure Island* and they called the kids onto the stage to take as much money out of the pirates' chest as you could carry. Chocolate money! We moaned all the way home. "Oh, I wish I'd known, I'd have brought a shopping bag. I'd have brought a suitcase!"'

'"I would have brought a whole lorry!"'

When they'd stopped laughing, Beth said, with something like wonder in her voice, 'Fancy you remembering all that.'

'Oh, I remember more than that,' An said, 'I remember everything.'

*   *   *

There's a cauldron in the middle of the hall. It squats on three legs, menacing black buffed to a dull shine. It blows steam on the mirrors, drips sweat into the crackling fire. Inside, water bubbles. Fox will have soup today. All he has to do is . . .

'Aha!'

You jump half out of your skin. His eyes glow yellow in the gloom. The table that you hide under is a cage of legs but you've been spotted and that's that. Fox has got you. He wraps a mangy arm around your throat and drags you out of the dining room, back to his lair, back to the simmering cauldron. You kick and scream and beg for your life, but it's no good.

'Even a fox must eat, my dear Raven. Into the pot with you, ha ha ha.' Rubbing his hands, chortling with glee, Fox scuttles off to find more prey.

'Skinflint. Oh, Skinflint, where are you hiding? Don't be afraid, my old, old friend. Fox would only like to talk with you. I have some soup all cooked and ready. Won't you join me for dinner?'

'It's a trick, it's a trick!' Trussed like a turkey, boiling nicely, you leap up and down, more in outrage than anything else. How can she be so stupid? Every single time – all Fox has to do is *lie* and out she comes, meek as a lamb.

'Oh, thank you, Fox. I am rather hungry.'

'And so am I, my dear, so hungry I could . . . EAT YOU UP! Into the pot with you. Have you met Raven before? I'm sure you'll both get along famously, once I put in the carrots and the onions and a little bit of stock. Lovely, lovely, lovely.'

Fox's eyes dance in his head. He prances around the cauldron, lets out an Indian whoop, getting his games mixed up. He thinks he's so clever.

'Well, I'm not playing anymore.' You shrug off the rope; with just a stamp of your foot, it evaporates. 'You always get us and you always cook us. It's boring.'

'That's what's supposed to happen. I'm Fox.'

'Why can't I be Fox?'

'Because you're Raven. An's Skinflint and you're Raven, so you get to be two things. That's why I get to be Fox.'

'Right, then, in this game the fire makes the water so hot the rope melts and when the fox is busy dancing and acting the fool, Raven lifts up her wings and flies away. She flies to the top of the highest tree and she watches to see what happens. And Fox is such a greedy fox that he eats up all the soup and doesn't even realise that it's only scrawny old Skinflint bones he's scrunching, and sour old Skinflint juice he's drinking. And he falls asleep, all cosy and stuffed by the fire, and when he's fast asleep Raven swoops down . . .' You leap into the air, knock Beth to the ground, 'and pecks out his eyes.'

Shoulders still steaming from the heat of her bath, An stood at the open window and watched Beth peg clothes onto the line. The green plastic rope sagged in a soft arc between a corner of the house and the shed their father had built at the end of the garden. Beth was about half way down, starting to hang a dark wash next to the perfectly sized and sorted whites. She worked slowly, methodically, moving inch by inch up the hundred-foot lawn.

Downstairs, a Bach fugue was playing. An waited till the goosebumps prickled through her skin again then she began to windmill her arms in time to the music. She swept her hands in ever increasing circles, keeping one eye on the glass shelves over the bidet. She had not remembered the room as this small. The pine cladding on the ceiling, varnished to a dark gloss, sloped down almost to her head.

It was best to sway from side to side whilst doing this stretch, visualising a slender tree in the wind, a mountain ash, a berry-covered rowan. But now she kept her trunk completely still, for fear of cracking her nails on the green-tiled walls. To compensate for this restriction, she took deep lungfuls of air, and blew them out through her nose like a horse. The music slowed, faltered, then came to an assertive halt in the minor key just as Beth tapped the last peg onto the last pair of panties. An said 'Abundant, abundant, abundant,' and finished her exercise.

The towel Beth had put out for her lay folded on top of the linen basket. She hadn't used it to dry herself; she preferred to air dry. Anyway, it was far too soft. What she really needed was a nice crisp flannel to rub over her skin. Mop up the last few remaining drops of water and get her capillaries going. Then she could finish up with some sweet almond oil and go and put her face on.

An looked around the bathroom: at the avocado-coloured bath, with its fresh ring of scum around the rim; at the basin and bidet; the green tiles inset with sunflower tiles. The Swedish-style ceiling and the thoroughly British deep-pile carpet. The glass shelves were cluttered with bath foams and salts in improbable shades of green and pink. Little soaps in the shape of hearts or bears. Jars of soluble bath balls. It looked as if Mummy had kept, unused, every Christmas and birthday present they had ever given her.

On the deep window ledge stood Beth's things. Rather more upmarket than Mummy's but functional at least. Clinique skin

care products, the little bar of caramel-coloured soap melting
in a puddle of water. Dior body lotion and deodorant, a pot
of dusting powder in a matching fragrance. An picked up each
item and sniffed it. She prodded a tube of depilatory cream
and a packet of waxed papers, rummaged her fingers through
the bag of multi-coloured cotton wool balls. Beth rarely used
make-up but she'd always prided herself on her flawless com-
plexion. Now she clearly had the money to use the best to
keep it so. The family purse again?

The bathroom reeked of girls together. A rail for Mummy's
towels and one for Beth's. A hook for Mummy's floral shower
cap, a hook for Beth's lace-trimmed one. So calm and femi-
nine. Sisterly, scented. She could almost see them in here,
giggling together while they titivated. Nothing like the bathroom she remembered. Beth and Mummy had erased the past
again with just a touch of paint here, a new accessory there.
The spoils of John Lewis stores and Selfridge's obscuring the
real house An knew to be just under the surface.

Everywhere, though, were little reminders, little subcon-
scious lapses. Here were Daddy's toiletries, marshalled on top
of the medicine cabinet, gathering dust. Colognes and after-
shaves and a box of English lavender soap. A leather case
containing his electric shaving kit. An ivory-handled brush
and a wooden bowl for wet shaving. His oval hairbrush. Daddy
had always had impeccable taste, an instinct for the finest
British craftsmanship. Beth had clearly inherited his subtle
eye for the expensive.

An reached up and grabbed the hairbrush. She had
Mummy's large hands; the smooth wooden base fitted neatly
in her palm. She weighed it there, looking at the sprigs of black
and grey hair enmeshed in the beaver bristles. She passed the

brush over her own hair. It was firm, unyielding, like the stroke of a bear's paw. Finally she raised the brush to her face and inhaled, deeply.

Sandalwood and Old Spice, lavender and shaving foam. A hint of the cigars Daddy had smoked when they were young. Sweat. Clean sweat. Man smells. For a moment, An was unsure which house she wanted to live in. The old one, where every item had a significance, a history. Or the new one: bright and modern, made over with his death money. Both, in a way, were his.

Well, if it was so easy, if all it took was a thin layer on the top to make everything alright, she'd go for the latter. An opened the airing cupboard and searched around on the warm dark shelves until she had found what she was looking for. A pair of matching duvet covers, in plain colours.

When she had dressed, An wandered down to the garden. Her morning chores over, Beth sat in her deckchair, an open book and a half empty glass of shandy on the plastic table in front of her. She opened her eyes as An's shadow fell across her face.

'Nice bath? Could you just move the umbrella for me, I'm roasting.'

An repositioned the umbrella, and flounced the frills as she'd seen Beth do. As she brought her hand away, she caught the edge of Beth's glass. Quickly, she steadied it, but not before some of the contents had slopped onto the table.

'You are such a clutz.' Beth had closed her eyes again. An couldn't tell if she'd seen her or had interpreted her sister's gasp of alarm.

'I'll get a cloth.'

'Don't bother. It will evaporate soon enough. Leave a nice sticky patch for the wasps.'

An hovered by the table, tapping a finger in the little puddle of shandy. She wanted to sit down but the second deckchair was folded on the grass and she didn't trust herself to set it up. On the other hand, she didn't want grass stains on her trousers before she'd even got out the front door.

Beth might have read her mind. She turned in her chair and said, 'What plans have you got for today, then?' just as An opened her mouth to ask if there was any more shandy. She shut it again, picked up Beth's book, pretended to read the dust jacket, closed it and put it down, strolled over to inspect the roses.

'Nothing really. I might just hang around here.'

'You've lost my page.' Beth kissed her teeth and rifled through the book until she found her place. 'You're very dressed up for hanging around.'

'Are you planning on doing this fence? I could give you a hand if you like. I love the smell of creosote.'

'Spoil your pretty trousers.'

'I didn't mean now.'

'Why not? If you're just hanging around . . .'

'Have I done something to upset you, Beth?'

'Don't be silly.' Beth stood up and made a minute adjustment to the umbrella. 'You're too sensitive, you are.'

'And you're not sensitive enough,' An muttered under her breath.

'What?'

An sat on the grass at her sister's feet. 'Look, is this about Greta? We haven't even mentioned her since I've been back. Yes, she is dead, she is gone but we need to talk about it, we can't just pretend . . .' An trailed off. She had entered taboo territory.

Beth would not meet her gaze; a pulse beat at the side of her mouth and at the mention of Greta's name her body grew stiff with tension. She stared over An's head at the roses then downed the rest of her drink in one long swallow. 'I'm getting another shandy. D'you want one?'

When she returned, An had set up the deckchair and was immersed in the final pages of Beth's novel.

Beth slid the glass across the table. 'How can you do that? The end is meaningless if you don't know the characters.'

'Oh, I like to cut to the chase, me.' She remembered her assertiveness training, took a deep breath: 'Speaking of which, yes, I am going out. I'll probably be out quite a bit. A lot of old friends to catch up with.'

'Steve Stine.'

'Stein, it's pronounced Steen. Yes, I'll be seeing Steve. Today in fact. We're meeting for lunch.'

Beth let out a long hissing breath from between her teeth. She looked at An.

'I don't know why you couldn't just say that in the first place.'

Because of this, An wanted to say, because you're always so judgemental and disapproving. Because you always treat me as if I haven't got two brain cells to rub together.

Beth was staring at her as if expecting an answer. She shrugged, a schoolgirl with nothing to say for herself. She tried not to look truculent.

'You're a big woman now, An, you're twenty-two. You know what you're doing. But just be careful. Remember what happened last time.'

8

Going to Meet the Man

The stains bloom like chrysanthemums on her chest, spreading out from the nipple, growing dark. Beth feels a tingling and a stinging and believes it's a punishment. Her breasts are withering. There will be no baby to suckle at them and they'll die, and then she'll die and it will be right and proper. She doesn't bother to look down.

Mummy ferries breakfast from the kitchen. Daddy's head is buried in *The Times*. They eat in silence as always. But the air is different, almost audible. Like a high-frequency scream, a secret close-mouthed grief.

An cocks her head, listening. She chews thoughtfully on a dumpling. Looks at Beth, sees: points.

'What's that on your blouse?'

Over at the council houses, a baby begins to cry. Beth claws at her buttons, suddenly feral, baring herself instinctively. She lifts up her head and the floodgates open. She never knew it spurted like that; a fine shower of breast milk spatters the table, milk and tears making music on the china plates. Mummy walks in from the kitchen and thumps a bowl of baked beans on the table. The beans dot white. At last it stops and Mummy looks at Beth. They all look at Beth, sitting half-naked in her usual chair.

'Good,' says Mummy. Her lip curls and she laughs. 'Good,' she says. 'Now you know what you've done.'

An stood next to the newspaper vendor at Embankment station and watched the passengers emerging into the lobby. People pushed through the ticket barrier in fitful swarms, billowing up from the tunnels and escalators, bringing the fug and rumble of the underground with them. Outside the sheltering arch, beyond the relentless streams of traffic and tourists, across the wide pavements and over a soot-blackened wall the Thames glittered in the late morning haze.

An thought about her back, exposed in a yellow halter top, and her backside, plump and peachy in striped cotton jeans. If, at this very moment, Stevie Stein was ambling down Villiers Street, would he recognise her? Would he gaze at her buttocks and murmur to himself, 'These we have loved'?

She was about to turn around when, for the third time in twenty minutes, she thought she saw him. She half stumbled forward, her face twisting into a smile of greeting and quickly out again. The stranger looked at her appraisingly, shook his head and wandered out into the sunny street.

It wasn't like Steve to be late. Maybe she'd got the days mixed up, that had happened before. Perhaps she should walk about a bit in case he was waiting in another gloomy corner, looking for her. But no, this was their usual rendezvous, he would know where she was. And although the station certainly was gloomy, it had mercifully few hidden corners. An tossed her head impatiently. Why did they always have to meet at Embankment, anyway? It was always so busy. It was

Steve's idea, of course. Their first meeting had been there, but apart from that it had little to recommend it. Drab, dusty, cold. The river was a plus, though, and Garfunkel's restaurant at the top of Villiers Street.

Embankment station, a walk by the river and a meal at Garfunkel's. The rituals of their romance. It was corny, like playing 'our song' on the juke box. She should have suggested they do something else, meet somewhere else. But she'd never forgotten the time they'd agreed to meet at King's Cross, the time she'd got the days mixed up. She'd waited for two hours, every second of that time expecting him to show. Until she couldn't take another leer or one more offer of 'work', and had run down the stairs to the underground and cried all the way home.

Sometimes it felt as though she'd spent the whole of her teenage years in tube stations, waiting for this man and for that. Stevie and, before him, Daddy. She would get in from school only to be sent straight out again to meet her father at Hendon Central. It wasn't fair; Beth's school was a twenty-minute walk away, An's an hour's bus ride plus a ten-minute walk. Beth was always home by the time she arrived, tired and hungry, yet it was An who was sent to meet Daddy. He needed her help to carry home the shopping.

Daddy worked in a large East End comprehensive and escaped to Petticoat Lane most lunch hours. There he bought tinned goods and fresh fruit: little jars of maraschino cherries past their sell-by date; slabs of stale fruit cake; German iced ginger biscuits; fig rolls – somehow they all tasted the same. Then there were the plastic wheels of sugared jellies, broken biscuits by the bagful, packets and packets of roasted peanuts. He said he was helping Mummy – the market was so much cheaper than the local shops. Actually, it was a perfect excuse for keeping her housekeeping money to a pittance.

They argued about it every month.

'You expect me to feed and clothe a family on this?' Mummy would shrill. She'd shake her fist, the crumpled notes clenched in her fingers. She knew better, though, than to give in to her urge to send the money flying round the room. The one time she had done that her contempt had quickly given way to panic. Daddy had got down on his knees and shuffled around the kitchen, retrieving every last note and coin. When he'd stood his face was a mask of calm. He'd looked almost cheerful.

'It's alright, darling,' he'd said. 'If my money's not good enough, it's alright.'

The 'darling' confirmed Mummy's worst fears. All month she begged him and every time he gave the same answer. 'No, darling. I wouldn't insult you with my poor sixty pounds.'

The next month she held on to the money. Sixty pounds. The sum never increased however much she complained. Shortly after An turned sixteen Mummy's complaints reached a new level of bitterness. Daddy released An from her duties, including helping him carry the shopping home. Without a helper the trips to Petticoat Lane were no longer viable. It didn't seem to occur to anyone to ask Beth, who was seventeen and getting ready for A levels. The 'cheap and nasty' food Mummy had scorned she didn't miss. It was the tinned goods and the fresh fruit that she now had to find the money for.

An began to pace, marching out into the sunshine and back into the shade. It was interesting, the way her eyes adjusted to the changing light. As she crossed the threshold of shadow, she was momentarily blinded. She practised opening her eyes wide each time then stopped as she realised how crazy it must look to passers-by. The heat and then the cool made her skin tingle. Maybe she'd be tingling anyway. The prelude to meeting Steve had always done strange things to her physiology. Would they even recognise each other? It had been over three years. Maybe he'd come and gone without seeing her. It wouldn't be the first time he'd got fed up waiting. Worst of all, what if Steve had seen her, known her and decided not to bother?

With a sudden tightening in her chest, fingers trembling, An pulled open her rucksack and felt for her compact. It had been her first grown-up present from her parents. The silver was tarnished now, the gilt decoration scratched away. It was light and smooth and comforting in her hand. As always, before twisting the clasp, she paused to read the inscription underneath. A mantra against self doubt. *To our dearest Anita, on the occasion of her 16th Birthday. May you always be the fairest of them all.*

Mummy's choice of words was ironic: An was the darkest member of the family, much darker than their honey-coloured mother; blue-black, like Daddy with his big, long-fringed eyes and thick eyebrows. Now she peered into the little oval glass and whispered, 'Mirror, mirror. Mirror, mirror,' again and again. She searched her reflection for flaws, checked her teeth for lipstick, her nose for stray snot. Noted for the zillionth time, and with enormous relief, that she had not inherited her father's nose. Finally satisfied that her beauty remained intact, she squeezed shut the compact, to find Steve's eyes smiling indulgently into hers.

Something borrowed, something blue; Mummy's M&S suedette jacket, Beth's jeans and high-heeled sandals. Oh, and

Daddy's old grandad shirt, fashionably outsized. Just a splash
of Charlie from the half-used bottle at the back of Mummy's
toiletries drawer. The brown leather handbag is yours, but
even that was a present, for your 17th birthday last month.
The only thing truly your own are the silky camiknickers,
cold and unfamiliar against your skin. You bought them last
Saturday with your C&A staff discount card. It feels lovely.
You hope he'll think so too.

Perhaps you shouldn't have worn it so soon. After all, you
hardly know each other, though you feel as if you've been
friends for ages. He certainly knows everything about you.
Well, nearly everything. It's easier in letters, of course. Easier
to be your real self.

His first letter to you, and the latest, are in your jacket
pocket, along with your silver compact. You've checked your
face, checked that you've got the date, time and place right.
Memorised, again, every nuance of the photo he sent with
the first letter. It's not a very good photo. Like yours, it's from
one of those photobooths. His face is slightly turned away
from the camera, his expression both bored and startled, as if
he was getting fed up waiting for the flash to go and was
starting to fidget when Click! One cheek is lit up, the other
in shadow. One of his eyes is closed. He's managed to get half
a smile in. His hair's standing up on end.

He's almost handsome. That's what Greta said when you
showed her the snap. 'Intelligent. And worldly-wise. He'll look
distinguished as he gets older. That's better than handsome
any day.'

To be honest, you'd quite like handsome. Someone to show
off, not just show-off about. But at least he's twenty-three,
miles older than the boyfriends of the girls at school. He

doesn't have to be handsome. He is a *man*. He . . . Steve . . . Steve's got nice brown hair, thick and chestnutty, slightly wavy. Steve's eyes are dark. Dark eyes are sexy. And he's working as a builder at the moment, until he goes to university next year, so he must be strong. Muscular.

Oh, this waiting is awful, you should never have been so early. Fashionably late would have been better, but, knowing you, that would have turned into outrageously late. At least this way you'll get to see him first. You can run away before he sees you. If you want to. If you have to.

But there's no time for any of that. Here he comes towards the ticket barrier, dense and square in black biker's leather. He never said he was a biker! Perhaps it's a fashion statement, covered from lapel to breast pockets in badges. Slogans, patterns and colours compete for space across his chest. His legs, in faded denims, strain against the metal gate. Mmmm, yes, he is muscular. His thighs struggle with the barrier then he takes the spewed, chewed ticket and shows it to the guard and is ushered past. He's not at all flustered. He's smiling, bright eyed, chirpy as a budgerigar. His hair still stands on end.

He catches your eye. He floats towards you, a helium balloon with a silly grin. He's wearing bright red bovver boots; he presents his feet like his best joke. And now he's inches away, proffering a hand, opening his mouth to speak. But you say it first; you've not waited nearly half an hour just for him to get the upper hand.

'Steve?' Disbelief squeaks in your voice.

He laughs. Deep, couldn't care less. 'Ani'a? Pleased to make your acquaintance.' He's holding your hand. Not shaking it, just holding.

'Y'know, your name won't do. It won't do at all. Not wiv a cockney accent. I'm going to call you Neets. Alright?'

His kiss was as she remembered it. Dry and pecking at first, then lingering, a little too wetly, his tongue reading hers like braille. An stifled a moan and braced her legs to stop them from trembling. His bare arms were warm and solid under her hands. She couldn't resist; she grazed through the short blond hair with her fingernails, stopping only when she reached the sleeves of his polo-shirt. He pulled away first. He looked at her with that kindly, satisfied expression. Avuncular. Proprietary. Damn. Strike one to Stevie Stein.

On their way out of the station, Steve leaned forward to throw a wave at the newspaper vendor. 'Alright, mate?'

The vendor nodded and muttered something An didn't catch, then the two men laughed. Steve was still chuckling as they walked into the gardens at Embankment Place. The grassy slope just inside the gate was garlanded with lovers. Around them, office workers, labourers, truants, mothers, strolled and lay in various states of undress, egalitarian in their worship of the English summer. An sneaked a look at Steve; he'd obviously been at it too. His hair was several shades lighter than she remembered, and he was just beginning to turn that shade of builders' bronze that she liked.

He took her arm and grinned at her. 'Neets, you're as sexy as ever. Fucking gorgeous.'

Upset at the private joke with the paperman, An retorted, 'And you, I see, are still playing the cockney gentleman. You can give it a rest now, Steve, this is me, remember.' She hadn't meant to sound quite so harsh. He stopped and looked at her, then looked around as if searching for something.

'Steve, where are you going?'

He was leading her across the lawn, around a flower bed, until they stood under a large tree. Next to them, its contents spilling onto the parched grass, was a large green waste paper bin. Discarded sandwiches, a half folded nappy, drinks cartons leaned in a precarious pyramid towards them.

'Oh, what's this, Stein's revenge? There's wasps all over that bin, I'll be stung to death. If the stink doesn't get me first.' An giggled. Then she frowned until her eyebrows met in the middle, and batted her hands at him, girlishly.

He pulled her round to the other side of the tree, and said, 'Now then. I'm pissed off with you. Where the hell have you been? Three years, Neets, for God's sake! And it was you who called me, remember? Yeah, well, I'm here now, and unless I'm very much mistaken, you're quite pleased to see me. So start acting it. I don't have time for messing about. I can always leave, right now if you want me to. The station's just over there.' He waited, one eyebrow raised imperiously.

'Oooh, you always were a bully. Kiss me again. Wet as you like.'

Steve stared. Then he threw back his head and laughed, revealing a blight of silver fillings. He had tiny pointed teeth. The teeth of a squirrel and the body of a bear. He hugged her happily, and she hugged him back. Suddenly she felt her eyes sting with tears.

I missed you too. God, I *loved* you, Steve.

For a moment An thought she had spoken aloud. Steve gave her a squeeze that squashed her to him, burying her nose in his neck. His skin was smooth and firm, smelling of soap and cigarettes and sun-warmed earth. She wanted to lick it, to trace the fine lines of his skin with her tongue, reading his surface like an ordnance survey map. She pulled his shirt out the back of his jeans and rested her hand in the small of his back. Cool here, and downy. He still wasn't sure, she could tell. They were twinned from the waist up, but below the waist he held himself apart from her. Just a little push, the tiniest prompt of her hand and he would press himself to her. And nudge one thigh between her legs. And cup her breast, not squeezing, only his thumb rubbing over her nipple. Then he'd kiss her mouth, deeply, forever. And then her eyes and her cheeks, and kiss all her tears away.

'Stevie?' she whispered.

'Mmmm?'

'Let's go and get some lunch.'

It was a perfect day for a walk by the river. They cut through the gardens, back onto Embankment and towards the station. Then they joined the throng of office workers crossing to and from the Royal Festival Hall, and added their footsteps to the ringing clatter vibrating through the narrow pedestrian walkway. The river was a dizzying drop away. It shone between the bars of the bridge and stretched off into the misty distance. Commuter trains rumbled back and forth. The noise was exhilarating at such close quarters. Glimpsed between the riveted struts of the railway bridge, the trains seemed to flash past, sleek in the sun.

An had forgotten how essential London felt in the summer, like it was the only place to be. The crowds in their primary colours, the school's-out kids with their chrome-plated ghetto blasters, eager-faced day-trippers, cameras held aloft. Everything was bright and shiny, but at the same time a fuzziness seemed to hang in the air. It was the pollution, of course, the accumulation of noxious fumes, the roads chocka with cars, tarmac melting in the sun. That was the rational view. All the same, the cloud that settled overhead gave the city a dreamlike quality. It did something to time, so that hours sludged sleepily past, while whole days unaccountably disappeared. Sounds were amplified yet muffled; traffic and laughter and ice-cream bells rose to a whispered omnipresent roar. And in the changed light, her head ringing, the jugglers and buskers and skateboarders became exotic, showing off their prodigious skills in a celebration of life, art and the season.

So suggested the enchanted gatherings of tourists, anyhow; as if these predictable acts of entertainment and money raising took place in no other city in the world. A cheer went up as a group of teenagers began breakdancing to the booming beat of a monster ghettoblaster.

'Stop a minute.' An linked her arm through Steve's and they paused to watch the boys, spinning and writhing on the concrete. Overhead, the sky was a flat, cloudless blue. Below them, the river lay sluggish and brown, exposing old wrecks and odd city flotsam buried in the mud beaches.

Steve bought sandwiches and two cans of ice cold lager and they leaned on the parapet overlooking the water. They ate their lunch almost in silence. When it was finished, Steve took the wrappers and lobbed them expertly into a nearby bin. He wiped his hands on his jeans and cracked open a can.

'So, Neets.' He squinted at her as he tilted back his head and gave a long swallow. Here it was; the questioning, the need for details, explanations. She waited, head bowed.

'You know, you don't have to tell me anything you don't want to. I can guess some of it, anyway.' His voice was low and gentle. He reached out a hand as if to touch her, then withdrew it.

'You're staying with your parents now.' It wasn't a question.

An locked her hands around her unopened drink and scurried frantically through the truth and some of the necessary lies, trying to decide which to tell him. He was right. She didn't have to say anything at all. She wanted to look at him, but her eyes were suddenly swimming with tears again. Turning away, she focused her attention on a riverbus, pulling across to the opposite bank in a swirling wake of muddy water.

'I missed you,' he said again. He was trying so hard not to ask, to let her know it was alright whichever way she chose. But if it had been the other way around, if it was Steve who had disappeared from her life for three years, she would want to know why.

'After I failed my A levels, they hardly let me out of their sight. It was school and back, school and back. I even had to give up my Saturday job. I didn't dare contact you.' She pulled the ring on her can and threw it over the parapet. 'It was terrible. After that . . . well, after that . . .'

'You got them in the end, though.'

'Got who?'

'Your A levels. You said in your letter that you were doing a degree. Funny you being in Sheffield. If I was still at Leicester Poly, I could visit you at weekends.'

An smiled. 'You still can.'

He nodded, trailing his fingers in the cold sweat from his can. 'Your parents,' he asked, 'how are they?'

'My Dad's dead: three months ago.'

'I'm sorry.'

An whirled around and gripped his arm. 'Don't say that, Steve, you know you don't mean it.'

'Oh, Neets, that was a long, long time ago. It doesn't matter any more what I think of them, or what they think of me. You're an adult now. You make your own decisions.'

'That's what Beth said this morning.'

'My Dad died as well, as it happens. Two years ago. Cancer.'

There was nothing she could say. Certainly not, 'I'm sorry.' An watched the people leaning out from the deck of the river-bus, and waited for him to speak again.

'Well . . . the student life must suit you, Neets, you really do look very well.'

'Oh, I've barely started all that,' An said brightly. 'I dropped out half way through the first year. I was ummm . . . ill.' She gave a hollow laugh. 'But I went back into the second year. No exams to repeat or anything, thank God. I'm doing alright. I start my final year in October. Yeah, I'm doing fine.'

An took several swigs of lager, and handed the can to Steve to finish. They resumed their walk, hands thrust into pockets. Eyes downcast, or appraising the scenery, but avoiding each other's gaze. It was cool now, in the shadow of the monstrous structures of the South Bank. Wedged between two concrete pillars, a figure crouched on a pile of blankets. Steve said, 'Wait,' and, leaving An, went to squat beside the man. They began a murmured conversation. An watched for a moment, then she went back into the sunshine and waited on a stone bench with her eyes shut and her face upturned.

When it came, Steve's kiss was light and unfamiliar. An opened her eyes and searched his face. He smiled at her, sadly she thought.

'Come on. Let's get back.'

Re-crossing Hungerford Bridge, she slipped her hand through his crooked arm and he patted her fingers. He seemed distracted. 'Who was that man?' she asked.

'I don't know. It was a boy. I'm doing residential in Newham now; you know, kids' home. He looked like one of my lads. He's only fourteen.'

An stopped, made as if to turn back the way they'd come. 'Shouldn't we . . . do something? Steve!'

'Do what?' Steve said. They were at the foot of the stairs leading up to the walkway. People squeezed past them, tutting with annoyance or silently pushing. 'We're in the way, let's go into the station.'

Steve strode straight to the ticket office. 'Single to Bethnal Green, please.'

'Steve?'

'Look, there's nothing we can do. He doesn't want money. He knows where Centrepoint is. I gave him some cigarettes. That's about the limit of my powers, I'm afraid.' He rubbed a hand over his face, wearily.

'What about us? It's barely two. I thought . . .'

'Sorry, Neets. I don't much feel like a lovely day out any more. I'll call you, yeah?'

He hugged her swiftly, and pushed through the ticket barrier. An stood and watched Steve's tousled head disappear into the crowd.

9

Notes and Queries

There's a black and white film, 1940s or thereabouts, Hitch-cock maybe; a noir thriller. In it there's a murderer, stalking women; a detective, stalking him; a beautiful, doomed heroine.

In the film someone – the hot-on-the-trail detective? – is searching a room, the heroine's or maybe it's the villain's, whatever. And at one point a cupboard door is opened, abruptly, to an orchestrated crash of music. There, on the inside, is a drawing – the murderer's unique signature. A dreadful, terrifying portrait of the intended victim, in which her black hair hangs about her face like dead snakes and her mouth is drawn back in a snarl. Her image leaps from the wood, flies out of the television screen and imprints itself on the retina.

The fright of it sent An bounding over the top of the sofa, shivering just out of reach of the cold blue light of the TV that flickered over the carpet. For months afterwards she felt the same flash of fear and heard the discordant, screaming music in the moment before she opened her wardrobe door. She always expected to see the Medusa face, as she called it, staring back at her in stricken surprise.

The last thing she anticipated when she opened her wardrobe door was the papers. They were bundled up and stuffed into a worn manilla envelope. Draped over them was the perished rubber band that had originally secured them. They were hidden under the summer clothes and the old blankets, amongst the outgrown frocks kept only for their nostalgia value. Discarded in a corner, gathering dust.

She'd been burying Beth's doll at the time – Greta's idea. Goldy, the blonde doll, had been the twins' best weapon of warfare since they were young girls. With her shiny, smiley face and blue eyes that actually blinked, she meant the world to Beth. Too old to play with dolls, she made clothes for her – whole outfits including hats and matching bags, out of the scraps from Mummy's sewing projects. If Goldy went missing, even for an hour, Beth was distraught. Banging on the bedroom door, alternating threats and screams, begging, or sagging listlessly to the carpet, her exhausted sobs provoking the twins to even greater malice.

'We're holding her hostage. We'll pull out a clump of hair every ten minutes. And Beth, *we* know that dolly hair doesn't grow back.'

Their demands were never unreasonable: half of that week's pocket money, a free loan of her best pullover, being nice for a whole week, or next time they'd kill Goldy. They never understood why Beth took so long to acquiesce. It was a simple trade-off; her doll's life for whatever the twins wanted. Sometimes, when she was hiding Goldy, An had to look twice at the doll's face, her round eyes clicking and blinking with every movement, to check that she really was just an inanimate plastic plaything.

The papers were dated 1976 through to 1979. Some of the letters referred to in them were clearly missing. The language was archaic but between the 'plaintiffs' and 'putatives', the 'grounds' and 'grievances', An was able to piece a story together. Daddy (our hero king) had been married before. He had a child, a legitimate son (the long-lost prince abandoned in the forest). He and the child's mother (the wicked step-mother) had separated early on. He left her (and went to seek his fortune). Greta thought he must be a bigamist. She looked it up in the dictionary; that would make him a criminal. That would be a secret he wouldn't want anyone to know. She took to checking his mail, steaming open letters on the treacherous breath of the kettle. His bedroom cabinet and the drawers of the tallboy came under close scrutiny. Between the leaves of every book in his bookcase might be clues. Daddy had murdered truth and she would find him out.

It wasn't till they showed the papers to Beth that it all fell into place. Daddy *had* been married before and had filed for divorce in '74. Beth would have been about ten months old, An not yet born. She unfolded the missing letters and spread them out on the bed. Her hand trembled, stroking the crumpled paper over and over again. She pointed out phrases, part obscured by the delicate flowers of dried tears. A daughter, another child on the way, but the machinations of the law were slow and it wasn't till 1982 that he was free to marry again. She had known for some time. A more diligent detective than her sisters she was attuned to the currents that flowed around their house, the things said and not said. Perhaps it was one of Daddy's jokes, literally to hide the skeletons in the closet.

Other families celebrate wedding anniversaries. Other families keep gold-cornered albums of photographs, or at least a little sheaf of pictures tied up with ribbon, where the bride smiles shyly up at him and the groom stares manfully into the camera, both of them so young, so thin you cannot believe they are the same parents you know. Other parents keep the story in a silk bag, to be pulled out and admired on special occasions. A catalogue of coincidence and near disaster, hilarious to them, boring to you, but you wouldn't have them not tell you. Not for the world would you miss the image of them hand in hand at the start, sure in the knowledge that love conquers all. Because whatever happens, however the years and the mortgage and the withheld promotions take their toll . . . whatever the snubs and sneers, the bitter tears, the promise remains; you might live happily ever after. They chose each other; they chose you.

You are not the millstone around their necks (although he says so). You are not the yoke that ties them together, the cause of their chafing and biting, the reason why the road is awash with blood. You are a princess, all of you princesses, born of love and pride and ambition. You know the story by heart; never could you be what this scrap of paper says you are – a bastard.

Beth opened the notebook and read the inscription on the inside front cover: *To My Dear Sister Greta, With Love, Always And Forever*. It was a new version of the journal An had kept as a child. Some of the passages were original, familiar from earlier readings. Others had been reworked, new information added, plus some poems. Like notes for an autobiography, Beth thought. The kind of thing a real writer, or someone with pretensions to being a real writer, might keep.

Underneath, in her clear rounded hand, An had made several stabs at a short poem. The page was littered with crossings out and scribbles, little sketches and abstract shapes. In the margin she had drawn tiny love hearts threading down the page on a line, like ivy. At the bottom right-hand corner of the page were four lines, neatly circled in red pen.

> Was I one then, or two?
> Was I me or was I you?
> What's the truth and what's a lie?
> If you lived, why did you die?

Beth shifted her bottom on the little padded stool and leaned her elbows on the dressing table. She tried not to catch her own eye in the mirror. The notebook had lain to one side for nearly an hour, reproachful in its plain grey cover, tempting her to condemn herself with a spill of face powder or an overspray of perfume. She had felt reckless, giddy, trawling her way through her sister's make-up bag while the book patiently waited. The battle was almost physical: her breath became laboured, her hands shook. Trembling, she had painted her nails and tried out a few more lipsticks. At last, she had cleared a space on the cluttered surface and spread the book open. Now she flicked through the pages and stopped at an entry in which she spotted her own name. It wasn't right, she shouldn't have to do this anymore, but it was essential she knew the score. She began to read.

It's a word game. Word association. Like the psychiatrist does in the black-and-white films where the woman's lying on the couch with one arm flung over her eyes and just her eyebrows and her agonised frown showing over the top. And she can't remember, she tries and tries but she can't do it, Doctor, it's just a blank, a horrible, empty . . . blank. And he says, we'll try again. Don't fight it. Don't think. Say the first thing that comes into your head.

We do it with names. We've got so many, different names for different moods. Like when Mummy's mad and she calls me Anita and the name cuts like her eyes do. Or Daddy's in a good mood and he says Nita, and it's like saying you're the best daughter in the world, a real princess.

We make name trails, all the names rolling into one another, rolling out of one another, no meaning, no angry or pleased, just words tumbling and reeling in little floods around your real name, round and back in circles. I'm Anita Nita Nisha Shama Ama An Anna An-boleyn An-bo B.O. Beth is Lisa-Beth Lisabeth Bethlise Bethel Bethlehem Thlemen Yeh-man Phlegmn Lemon. We choose the name we like the best, the name we want to be that day. Today we're B.O. and Phlegmn. Don't let Daddy hear us.

Mummy says we're disgusting. She says, why must unu have so many names, I can't keep up? Like in *War and Peace*, where everyone has at least two names and you have to keep flicking back through the pages to check that so-and-so is the handsome young soldier also known as . . . Why can't you be like the Golightly girls, 'the kids'? They have only one name each, Dette and Dap. Dap and Dette. She says, better they'd stuck to C and D. D 'n' C. Either way sounds like a surgical procedure; a dapendectomy. Or a dilatation a curettage. It's a nurse-thing, she says, we wouldn't understand. Maybe she played this game too, Back Home with her sisters.

Mostly we're An-bo and Lemon.

We haven't worked out a name trail for Greta yet. Maybe it would start Margareta Greta Grater Regretter.

'Coo-eee!'

Beth, dozing in the garden, was awoken by a high-pitched voice and the sound of someone banging on the passage gate. She stumbled to her feet, dizzy in the intense light. She almost tripped on the cold box, righted herself and crossed the lawn to the path.

'Who is it?'

'It's only me. Claudette.'

'Dette? What are you doing in the passage?' Beth fumbled with the padlock sleepily, then remembered the key, hidden under a half brick beside the bins. 'Hold on. Just a tick.'

'I've been ringing the bell for ages. Then I thought you'd probably be sunning your carcass out back. You ladies of leisure, I don't know.'

Beth held the gate open and Claudette Golightly, one of her oldest friends, pushed past her into the garden, wafting cologne and daisy print cotton. Claudette picked her stilettoed way across the lawn and they settled themselves in the deckchairs. Beth had moved them under the apple tree, which afforded more reliable shade. The table and umbrella and

matching garden chairs now lived on the patio, so she and
An could take their breakfast there in the mornings.

'Ah, this is nice. Your Mum keeps the garden lovely.'

'Oh, I do most of it these days. My only creative outlet,
apart from the sewing.'

'Aren't you going back to work?' Dette eased off her shoes,
leaned forward and lifted the lid off the cool box. She smiled
when she saw the pitcher of shandy and a plastic beaker,
tucked in amongst the white grapes and a tub of melted ice-
cream as if it had been waiting for her.

'I don't know. The job in Harrow has well and truly gone.
I told them I wasn't coming back as soon as Daddy got his
diagnosis. You know I never did get my wage rise, and they
gave that new designer the denims contract after they'd
promised it to me. The cut-throat world of the cut cloth world,
eh. That's shandy, by the way. Beer. Beware all ye Christians.
Anyway, I can't decide if I should stay here with Mummy, or
retrain, or travel.'

Dette sipped at the shandy and made a face.

'There's more lemonade indoors if you want it.'

She was up and padding towards the house before Beth
could stop her. 'I'm on the case,' she called over her shoulder.
When she came back, Beth had put on a pair of sunglasses
and was rubbing oil into her limbs to stop the sun drying her
skin out. She was iridescent from head to foot.

'Scared of getting a tan?'

'I think it has got some UV something or other in it.' Beth
peered at the bottle, trying to read the small print without
taking off her glasses. 'Oh well,' she dropped the bottle into
the shadows. 'Smells nice anyhow.'

'Don't you get bored, being out of work for so long?'

'Dette, it's not as if I've been sitting around twiddling my thumbs. He needed twenty-four hour care for the last six weeks, and almost that for the last year.'

Dette had the good grace to look embarrassed. She was a nurse, after all, like Mummy. She knew how messy, how laborious and all-consuming death could be.

'Of course; you're having a holiday yourself now. Looks like it's going to be a perfect summer for you.'

Beth sighed. She took off her sunglasses and wiped the bridge of her nose with a tissue. 'I'm not sure how much rest I'm going to get though. Now Anita's back.'

It wasn't anything specific. She didn't leave her underwear lying around, or forget to clean the bath. If she made herself a drink she would always ask Beth if she wanted something. She would do her share of the cooking and cleaning, if Beth let her, and she didn't make excessive use of the telephone. She remembered to let Beth know when she was going out, and with whom. She made cheerful conversation and never borrowed any of Beth's things without asking.

But Beth found herself exhausted at the end of every day in a way she never was when Daddy was ill. Give her a death watch and a dirty bedpan any day. That was just physical, graft and vigilance. Being with An required something altogether different. Something that no one else had ever required of her, but An somehow always had. There wasn't a word for it. It was more a collection of vague feelings. A sense of unease, an ache behind the eyes.

An had always been complex, not as a very little girl but from around the age of seven. There'd been unrest of some sort at primary school, Beth remembered. She never knew the full details; it was not the sort of thing her parents discussed openly, but she'd heard whispers. During her last year at St John's, before she went on to comprehensive, whenever she did something pleasing, the teachers would say: 'Such a sensible child. So grown up and stable and reliable . . .' Then they'd add darkly: 'How two children from the same family could be so different is a mystery.'

As a teenager, things had gone from bad to worse. An seemed to settle at the grammar school but there were endless dramas at home; An was usually at the centre of them, if she wasn't the cause of them, egged on by Greta. The two of them became indistinguishable in their wilful fury. She'd started seeing Steve, failed her A levels, mercifully passed the resits. Even after An left to go to Sheffield Poly she came home every weekend. When she'd ended up in the hospital at the age of nineteen, Beth had been glad. Not that An was crazy, that she was suffering, but at least the screaming was out of earshot. She didn't have to feel she was entering a war-zone every time she came round for Sunday lunch. How Mummy had stuck it for so long she had no idea.

And Daddy! Now, if Beth had behaved that way around Daddy – swearing, and fighting and carrying on. Well, it didn't bear thinking about. He simply wouldn't have tolerated it. Wasn't that the way it always had been? Beth scurrying around doing as she was told, doing everything right. A levels, degree, job, never going further than the next borough, always on hand if needed. And she had been needed and her parents had never thanked her for being there, not in so many words. She didn't mind that. What Beth really minded was the way An got away with murder. Was even rewarded for it.

'She's out of hand,' Beth used to complain. 'Why are you – why is Daddy – letting her get away with it?' But Mummy wouldn't meet her eye and wouldn't give a proper answer. Always some nonsense about An being gifted and highly strung. She needed special encouragement, special consideration.

Take the boxroom. Beth should have got the boxroom, she was the eldest. It had been promised to her first but every year the promise receded. It wasn't even as if they needed a guest room, they hardly ever had staying guests. Mummy just liked the idea. Mummy leafed through the women's magazines and dreamed of fringed bedspreads with matching valances and contrasting curtains. She bought fabric swatches and paint charts, laid them out on the kitchen table like a hand of patience. Stood scratching her chin and cocking her head from side to side, asking Beth's opinion and dismissing it with a grunt. Meanwhile, the room stayed spartan and unused.

Then, when An was sixteen, some kind of deal was struck. Beth knew it, she just *knew* it. Why else were the three of them so pleased with themselves? Why else did An get the boxroom? There was a price, and Beth was astonished at how readily An agreed to pay it. She had turned her back on Greta without a moment's hesitation. In return she got the boxroom and a free rein. Greta left home; for a time they thought she was dead. In any case she disappeared for a year, only to resurface with a stronger hold on An. More destructive, more determined.

'I love her to bits, you know that. And I was really frightened for her when she . . . went away. When she got better, and with Greta gone and everything, I begged and begged her to come home if only for a visit, a weekend even. I just wish she could have found a way to make her peace with Daddy . . .

Now it looks like she's going to do the same thing with Mummy too.' Beth closed her eyes. Suddenly she burst out, 'And I'm sick of being piggy in the frigging middle.'

Overhead, an aeroplane droned, sounding too low in the silence, on its way into Heathrow. From over the fences, in another garden, came the sound of laughter and a dog yelping. Somewhere else, someone else screamed, 'Fucking shut up.' A door banged. The motorway hummed ceaselessly.

'Where is Anita, by the way?' Claudette looked around the garden as if expecting An to materialise from behind the runner beans.

'She's seeing that white boy. Steve.'

'The one from . . . ?'

'The very same.' Beth propped her feet up on the cool box and crossed her ankles.

Dette touched her friend's knee conspiratorially. 'She still doing that Greta business?'

'That had nothing to do with it. He was the one who set her off in the first place, I should have told Mummy about him from the beginning. God knows what those two used to get up to. An was never easy, to say the least, but after Steve came along . . .'

'No, I don't remember it like that. If you'll forgive me saying so, that girl was on the slippery slope from about eleven. Anyway, what is it you disapprove of: his himness or his whiteness?'

'Neither. His face, broad as a shovel and twice as thick. But if you'll forgive me saying so, it's not your family to remember. She's my sister. As I recall, you were none too fond of him yourself.'

'He had some things going for him, though.'

'Like?'

'Education. He was putting himself through evening class and about to go to college, yeah? And, erm, well, education and education. How should I know? Maybe he's hung like a German sausage.' Dette laughed.

Beth didn't. 'He was no good for her. He didn't treat her right. Do you remember that time we all went to the fair at Hampstead Heath? Those two, me and George, you and Peter and Dap. Dap must have been between boyfriends, as usual. Anyway, Steve and An went off, d'you remember that?'

'Yeah, and it was obvious they'd been doing the nasty behind some bush or something. Her blouse was done up all wrong and he was grinning like the cat with the cream. Your Mum'd have a fit if she knew he was back on the scene.'

Beth looked at Dette warningly. 'She's not going to find out.'

'So you haven't been getting on?' Claudette said carefully. Her voice dripped with sympathy.

Beth bristled, immediately on the defensive. 'Well, it's only to be expected, our Dad's just died, on top of everything else. There's been a lot of upheaval recently. No. No, it's totally overstating the case to say we're not getting on . . .'

'You just have to get to know each other again,' Dette finished for her. 'I know, Beth. I have seen this kind of thing before. Through my work. Often after a breakdown, people are changed. Unpredictable.'

Beth studied her, trying to decide something. Then she took Dette's hand and pulled her to her feet. 'I want to show you something.'

Upstairs, Beth led the way into the back bedroom. An had replaced the Pierrot quilt covers with two even older ones, pink on one side and brown on the other. She had taken all the books out of the bookcase and stacked them under the unused bed. Her shoes – stilettos, clogs, strappy sandals, gleaming new trainers and a lone chinese slipper – stood to attention on the shelves. The dressing table was covered with dozens of tiny jars and crumpled tubes, the entire contents of An's make-up bag. Little spills of brown powder and smears of lipstick coloured the varnished wood. She had laid out all her outfits on both beds, as if she'd agonised over what to wear that day.

'P-lease,' Dette sniffed the air, thick with the scent of freesias and An's perfume. 'It looks like Madonna's dressing room in here. How long is she staying?'

'Never mind that. Look. What do you make of these?' Beth got down on one knee and fished under the bed. When she stood up she was holding a bottle of pills in one hand and a spiral-bound notebook in the other. She looked at the notebook, then she shook her head and pushed it back into the farthest corner, where it was hidden by the valance.

'What are those?'

'I was hoping you could tell me.'

Dette studied the label. She weighed the bottle in her hand, trying to guess how much had been used. She unscrewed the lid and peered inside without touching the little capsules. Then she put the lid on and handed the bottle back to Beth.

'The name's not entirely familiar, but it does ring a bell. I'm fairly sure it's a heavy duty sleeping pill they dish out in hospital. The drugs industry make minute changes to the compounds and bring them out under different names. They're road testing them all the time really. On the market. I could look it up in my *Mimm's* if you like.'

'Thanks, Dette. I see pills and I start to panic. Y'know, after Greta. I just want to know what I'm dealing with.' Beth was glad Dette didn't ask her how she'd come to find the pills in the first place.

10

Texas Street Blues

Once upon a time there were three billy goats gruff who lived high in the mountains. There they had mountain grass for grazing, the air was sweet and crisp and there was always clear cold water to drink from the mountain streams. The billy goats, however, were dissatisfied. From their home they could see a nearby pasture where the grass was always lush, green and plentiful.

'If only,' they lamented, 'we could go into that pasture and taste the grass,' and their mouths watered at the very idea.

To get to the field they had to come down from the mountain and cross a river. There was a little wooden bridge that led over the river but underneath the bridge lived a terrible troll. Whenever anyone tried to cross over to the other side, he would leap out from his hole in the river bank and gobble them up.

One year there was a particularly harsh winter. By the time the spring came there was no grazing to be had in the mountains.

'We shall have to venture down into the pasture,' said the goats to one another, then they argued amongst themselves as to who should go first and face the terrible troll. Eventually the biggest goat said, 'I am big and I am strong. I am easily a match for that old troll.' So off she went; tip-tap tip-tap over the bridge. But the troll leaped out and gobbled her up. Then the middle-sized goat; tip-tap tip-tap over the bridge, but the same fate befell her. The littlest billy goat gruff saw what had happened. She was not as strong or as fierce looking as the rest of her family and she was very afraid, but she was also very hungry. She decided to set off for the pasture and on the way down the mountain she would think of a plan to outwit the troll.

Nothing comes to mind.

You can hear Beth singing in the kitchen, pop songs and washing up. Mummy's in the bathroom, having a bath. You're washed and dressed and ready to come out of your room but the troll's waiting and you can't see your way past him.

Saturday morning. He lies on the landing in his string vest and Y-fronts. Dozing in the multi-coloured sun coming through the stained glass window. Reds and greens burn bright on his skin. Head by the toilet door, feet hanging over the stairs, he rests on his back. You know and he knows. He's not sleeping. Lazy hand moves down his body, pauses and returns. His elbows make a V, hands behind his head. Opens one eye. In the white Y, yawning like an abyss, something lolls and dangles. Black, very black, and shiny. Heavy looking. Slick and curved.

Crouching, you take a step, drawn to it, stop. He can make it twitch and dance, stretch and stand, no hands. He does his party trick, red eye watching you. Winks. The river roars in flood, ready to burst its banks. You are deafened, drowning.

'Bernard! Cover yourself up.'

He feigns slow awakening. 'You finished in the bath yet?'

'You should have knocked, I finished from time. I was only titivating.'

Mummy makes to step over him. Biggest billy goat gruff, fearless with her big horns and her bellow. Troll can't catch her. Then she sees you on all fours by the bedroom door. She looks at Bernard, back at you, at Bernard again.

'Anita. Get downstairs.' A hiss; two cut-eyes. Daddy doesn't move. As you step over him and start down the stairs her hand meets the back of your head and sends you skidding to the bottom.

11

The Kids

'An? An, get your carcass in here.'

As soon as she opened the door, An heard music and laughter. She'd recognise those voices anywhere. Her instinct was to turn and run, but she'd already spent enough hours kicking around the West End. She must have browsed through every shop on Oxford Street, strolled the crescent of Regent Street down to Piccadilly and back again half a dozen times. She'd tried three McDonald's and a Burger King, stringing out her meal like a restaurant critic at a French feast; milkshake near Tottenham Court Road, fries at Oxford Circus, quarter pounder at Marble Arch and back down the other end of the road for a hot pie and coffee. An unexpected shower had driven her from Hyde Park. The mysteries of Soho had not appealed. There was nowhere else to go, besides, what possible excuse could she give for coming home and immediately going out again?

Beth should have told her 'the kids' were coming. She checked her face at the oval mirror in the hallway and arranged her features into the appropriate expression of delight. Not too happy; she must look self-composed, grown-up. Seeing the kids again would be a test of her rehabilitation, the hours of therapy, the drugs. Just as Polytechnic was. And coming back to the homestead. And seeing Steve.

None of it was going according to plan. Maybe she'd waited too long to be ready. Perhaps if she'd come sooner they would have had more time for her. Greeted her with protestations of love, tokens of their regard. Apologies. Beth had made an effort, it was true. The nice meal and the flowers and everything. But after that she had seemed impatient, as if An's presence was an irritation, disturbing the calm waters of the life she'd made for herself.

As for Steve, he'd literally walked away. She was not as interesting as the boy under the bridge. Not as worthy a cause. Really, it was as if the hole An had surely left by her absence, had undergone some rapid healing process. The layers of people's lives had simply grown around the gap, until now there was hardly any room left for her at all. She raised an eyebrow at herself, and saw her face and the back of her head reflected into infinity by the mirrors on their opposite walls. Then she strolled into the front room.

'The kids', Daphne and Claudette Golightly, looked up from the recesses of the armchairs as she walked in. Just a year between them, and the same age as An and Beth respectively, they were like their alter egos. Their mother had known Mummy for years, all four girls had gone to the same primary school, An and Daphne starting in the same class just as Beth and Claudette before them.

As little children, the younger girls had been inseparable. Mummy used to joke: 'I've never seen two babies who can't yet talk have so much to say to each other.' Nita and Nep would sit in the back garden with their arms around each other and giggle all day long given half a chance. An didn't exactly remember them, but the stories of their infant exploits had been told so often she had vivid pictures in her mind of two plump girls, one dark one bright, each mouth against the other's ear, whispering, whispering.

Due to some administrative adjustment, they'd been put in different classes at the age of eight. An's bonds with her old classmates were virtually severed overnight, but the friendship with Daphne should have endured. They lived not five minutes away from each other; Mummy and Daddy approved; Mrs Golightly was like an aunt to An. Instead it faded, year by year, inexorably. Then An got a place at the grammar school – Daphne joining Claudette and Beth at the local comprehensive. For An it would have been a dream come true if they had managed to get together, circumnavigating Daddy's restrictions to create new, more daring, teenage exploits. But of course, life wasn't like that.

Claudette jumped up at once and rushed to hug her. 'Woy, Anita, you're looking great. Isn't she, Dap? Oh, it's so good to see you. Stacked and fit. A bit margar, but I reckon you're going to beat Lisa-Beth here in the heritage stakes.'

She meant An's backside. It was a habit she'd picked up as a teenager, referring to people's anatomy in salacious terms. It was in odd contradiction to her nature. Claudette was as serious, as moral and devout as anyone An had met. A confirmed Christian since secondary school, she had married her childhood sweetheart, Peter, about eighteen months ago. An was sure Claudette had been a virgin until the very day.

'Dette, stop it, you're embarrassing the girl.' Dap rose slowly to her feet and approached An shyly. 'Hey there, sis, we missed you.'

'Me too, Dap. It's been a long time.'

As restrained as her sister was extrovert, Dap held An's hands in hers and smiled at her.

'We're hitting the vodka. Well, some of us,' said Beth, grimacing at Dette, 'D'you want one?' She waited expectantly beside the drinks cabinet, the red interior light twinkling off the massed bottles and lighting up her skin.

'Nah, not my tipple. But is that Canei I spy?'

'Party girl!' said Dette. 'Is that all they teaching you at Univer-sa-tay?'

'Oh shut up, you.' Beth's familiarity surprised An. She hadn't realised the kids and her sister were so close. As far as she was aware, they'd all lost contact years ago. But of course, Beth had never been far from the homestead, and Mrs Golightly still lived just down the road. Beth and the girls would buck up whenever they were in town. There was certainly no-one else around here her sister would bother with.

'Dette's just started her Master's,' Beth explained, 'so don't let her come the bumpkin with you. That woman is a dyed-in-the-wool, true-blue member of the Black Intelligentsia.'

'More power to you,' they choroused and raised their glasses to a blushing Dette, squirming in her armchair.

An settled herself in a corner of the sofa, next to Beth, and took several small sips from her glass. The ice bounced gently off her lip and sent syrupy swirls through the pale liquid. Outside it was starting to cool but the evening was still bright and balmy. There was something soothing about sitting with old friends, drinking adult drinks as day gave way to night. Listening to the Robbie Vincent show on the radio, all the soul classics. Like the times she had in Sheffield with her mates from the Debating Society, or the dinner parties her friend

Eloise hosted. Times like this, An knew she had arrived. She
had finally broken through, left all the mess of the past behind.
Begun a new phase in her life where she had as much to offer
as anyone else. Where she was indistinguishable from anyone
else.

'So what's your thesis, have you decided yet?'

'Well, I'm still nursing, and really all this study is just to
further that career. I'm interested in looking at black women's
experience in the mental health system in terms of access to
services, diagnoses, etcetera. I'm particularly interested in the
kind of creative strategies people use in times of stress, and at
what point these mental safety valves become mental illness.
I'm already in danger of getting immersed in the sociological
aspects so I have to bump up the clinical side but that's mostly
bookwork, I can bluff it.'

Claudette's tone had become briskly formal, her slight Trini-
dadian lilt undetectable as she talked about her work. An
thought, Daddy used to do that, and Mummy to a lesser
extent. If they were chatting to family or close friends (black
friends) their accents relaxed, broadened, the rhythm and
timbre warming the air. It was an almost physical change.
Like shrugging out of an ill-fitting coat and rolling up your
shirt sleeves. But in public – when ordering something in a
shop or discussing a daughter's progress at parents' evening –
they became high-pitched and clipped. Coming over all speaky
spokey. Daddy's nasal whine was practically a parody of the
Queen's English. It had the same effect as nails screeching
down a blackboard; it made you cringe and want to cover
your ears.

Claudette wasn't as bad as that, of course, and presumably
she wasn't doing it in an attempt to show breeding. An

wondered if she even realised that her voice had changed. It was a bit like the one Mummy used for white friends and neighbours; an accommodation between the two accents was reached. Mummy was good at this, having more to do with local acquaintances, and generally being more sociable. But for Daddy, who all day was Mr B. Moore, English teacher extraordinaire, attempts to take his accent down just a notch without lapsing into 'home' talk usually made his (and everyone else's) eyes water. He just couldn't do it. His tone would peak and trough, peppered with eh hems, aarrrmms, and catarrhal coughing. Finally he would take refuge in taciturnity, and Mummy would pass him off as shy.

'But look,' Dette was perched on the edge of her seat, her face glowing with enthusiasm. 'How long are you home for? Maybe we could talk? I need to do some case studies and I'd love to know more about your experiences with Greta ... What? What have I said now?'

An fixed her eyes on her lap. Beth and Dap were looking daggers at Claudette.

'Well, it's not a secret, is it? We all know what Anita's been through. I think this whole twin thing is fascinating and really, it's much healthier to discuss these things. There's absolutely nothing to be ashamed of, An.'

'Claudette! Enough!'

'You have no idea, Claudette . . .' Beth and Dap spoke at the same time.

An swallowed a heavy sigh and finished her drink in one gulp. She looked Dette straight in the eye and said steadily, 'No, it's alright. Dette's absolutely right. Why not use my experience? It's got to be good for something, after all.'

She laughed. There was a long embarrassed silence. Outside,

the sky was turning to navy blue high up, with a thick band of yellowy cloud below. An got up and poured herself another drink. She turned her back on the others and added ice from the bucket Beth had placed on the open lid of the drinks cabinet. Someone else was going to have to play peacemaker. After all, no-one had asked her if she was ready for guests.

She took her drink over to the window and stood gazing out. The net curtains fanned her face, calmed her. She would have liked someone to stand beside her. Just put their arm around her waist. Maybe let her rest her head on their shoulder, and stand with her, quietly, in the soft breeze of the evening. Times like this, she wished Greta was still with her

A woman's voice purred, in the silken tones of radio-land: 'Music for a candle-lit dinner.'

They recovered quickly, smoothing over the hitch as people who have known each other a long time can. In response to Dap's questioning, An explained that she was studying English at Sheffield Polytechnic. Yes, her Dad had 'done' Literature at Oxford. No, she was not following in his footsteps. He had gone on to do a Master's in Education. She would probably be a social worker, never a teacher. She was just back for the summer, keeping Beth company while Mummy and Auntie cruised. They all laughed at this notion: the two merry widows whooping it up in the ballroom, sunning themselves on deck, knocking back the rum punch.

Mrs Golightly had done a similar thing when her husband had passed on. Although he hadn't got as far as the other side – just another bed. He'd taken up with a girl only five years older than Dette. Mrs Golightly had been hard pressed, left to raise two young teenagers on her own. But she'd managed to scrape enough money together for a four-week trip home, to Trinidad and Tobago.

'Dette and me were shipped off to these cousins in Ealing. They were grim. Cornmeal porridge *every* morning. And church five times a week. That's how Dette got so devout.' Dap leaned over and jooked her sister on the side of her head. 'Mashed up her brains.'

Dette smirked quietly to herself, twirling between her fingers the little gold crucifix she always wore.

'We missed Ma like mad, though. You know how easy going she always is. It was a total culture shock to be, like, living in the house of the Lord.'

Her sister gave Dap a warning look; she was going a bit far now. Besides, An and Beth already knew this story. But Dap was just easing the way for her next probe. It might go a little easier if proceeded by a tickle.

'It's a real shame you didn't get to see your mum before she went on her trip. She was saying to Ma how she was really looking forward to seeing you. I can't imagine not seeing Ma for two whole years. Four weeks was bad enough.'

'Mummy's not like your Ma,' said An.

'Isn't she?' Dette asked. 'I think she's cool, actually. I really like talking to her. She gives some good advice too. Anyway, she's still your Mum.'

'So I've got a duty to her. I owe her or something.'

'Yes! Yes, you do.' Dette was scandalized. 'Honour your mother and father . . .'

'But what about the duties that parents owe their children?' It was practically a shout. Everyone turned to Beth in surprise. Two bright spots of colour had appeared beneath her brass coloured skin. She sat with her feet tucked under her, resting her empty glass on her knees. Her hands were gripped so tightly around it the knuckles were pale. Her dark purple nails stood out in marked contrast to them. It looked to An just like the varnish she had on her dressing table, liver coloured with a glittery sheen.

'It's an old cliché, but think about it for a minute,' Beth continued. 'Children don't ask to be born. They don't decide to be here, they don't have any choice. How can they owe anything?'

An got up and collected everyone's glasses for a top up, then put the rest of the Canei, the vodka and mixers on the table. The ice bucket was nothing but water now, but all attention was on Beth. Ice could wait.

'This is in the bible also.' Beth looked at Dette. '"As you sow, so shall you reap." If you don't invest real love and attention and respect ... Yes, respect for your children! It's a two-way street you know. Our parents can't expect it without earning it.'

'But what about all the other things they invest in? All the hard work that goes into raising us? Kids ain't easy you know. And they're not cheap. And as black people, our parents had a lot to contend with in this country. They came here at a time when people were still putting notices in their windows, "Room to let, no dogs, no Irish, no niggers." Except maybe the polite ones said "No coloureds", but the message is the same.'

'You're all over the place now, Claudette,' An broke in. 'What is your point?'

'My point is this.' Dette spoke slowly and carefully, as if explaining something to a very young child. 'Not one of us knows what it is to be a parent. By the time they were my age, both our Mas had had their first child. Because of our parents' hard work and sacrifice we've had the luxury of decent schooling, higher education, the chance to do better than them. Every one of us has at least an HND. Without our parents, and the encouragement they've given us, especially our Mas, we could not have achieved that. Of course we owe them a duty. They may not always have got it one hundred per cent right. Maybe they were weak sometimes, or too strict. I know your Dad could be a bit handy, and our Dad . . . Well we know about him. But they had pressures on them that we can barely imagine. It's just old stories to us, but it was their lives. My point is, they raised us as best they could, and we've all done alright from it. We're still here, with all our limbs intact and everything, still with our eyes on the prize. Yes, we owe them a duty. And I pray to God my children feel the same way when I've raised them.' Dette sat back in her chair, well pleased with herself, to murmurs of dissent from the others.

'Speachify, testify,' teased Dap.

'That's one version,' said Beth.

'A bit handy!' An muttered. 'Girl, you don't know the half of it.' She hadn't intended to be heard but when she glanced up from her drink she caught Beth looking at her strangely.

'OK,' An said. 'Let's try this for size. A child comes into the world. Black or white, rich or poor, it's there because its parents decided it would be. It's a serious thing to bring a child into the world. From that point on, they owe the child everything. It needs understanding and love and patience if it's to grow well. Everyone talks about parental rights. Well, I don't think parents have a right to beat their children when they could just as easily talk to them. I don't believe parents should bully their children; support, encourage, provide, but at the end of the day, a child has to be its own person. And if you set up an "us and them" in the family, like Mummy and Daddy did, with kids on one side and parents on the other, why the hell should we all be friends together when the kids are grown up? It can't work that way. Like Beth says, "What you sow, so shall you reap."'

Dap said, 'That argument only works if you suppose that everyone has equal access to contraception, and we know that ain't so. Lots of parents don't have choice, anymore than kids do. Yours and mine certainly didn't.'

'Yes, but why is it so unreasonable to expect them to take responsibility? At the end of the day, they're the adults.'

'They did, didn't they, take responsibility?' Beth looked puzzled, as if she couldn't make up her mind which camp to be in. 'They fed us, clothed us, put in central heating. Got you into grammar school, An, when Miss Tart said you weren't clever enough. She was all ready to recommend that the head-mistress reject you. Mummy stopped her: doesn't that count for something?'

Dap clapped her hands. 'Fair's fair, Beth. I think An got herself into grammar school. She took the test. No-one did that for her.'

'Thank you, Dap.' An boggled her eyes at her sister. 'Make up your mind, Beth. Stop contradicting yourself. Anyway, what I'm saying is, there's more to it than that. Love, respect, remember?'

'What do our parents' generation know about all that?' Dette laughed. 'Our Dad used to give us some wicked beatings. They were brought up on "spare the rod, spoil the child". Talk to us? You must be joking. I remember one time . . .'

'Why is that funny?' Beth interrupted. 'You know, An's right. I'm sick of laughing about this thing. Beatings are scary. And they hurt. I've got the scars to prove it.'

'Ah, come on.' Dette shook her head and poured herself a tonic water. 'We survived.'

'And surely your mum wasn't like that?' asked Dap, persisting with her original line. 'I mean, she always seemed lovely to me. Aren't you blaming her for your Dad's failings?'

An huffed and heaved herself around in her seat. It was hard to sit still. She wasn't used to having these kinds of conversations outside of her therapist's office. Usually it was she herself who took both parts of the argument, battling with herself and her upbringing. Sylvia just nodded and let her run. Literally sometimes, up and down the office, the energy of her words compelling her to motion. She unfolded her legs and straightaway curled them under her again.

Dette suddenly assumed a cunning, self-satisfied expression. 'Yeah, and you supposed to be a feminist, too.'

'There's no "supposed to" about it.'

'Some feminist, blaming the woman. Not just any woman, mind, a black woman, a mother. She raised you against the odds. Did the night shift from the time you were two. Wiped the shit off strangers' arses – pardon my French – so you could eat and go to grammar school and swan off to university.'

'Polytechnic.'

'Same difference.'

An and Claudette were sizing up for a fight, staring at each other with baleful intensity, bodies slumped deceptively in their respective seats in a pretence of cool. Their sisters looked from one to the other, like spectators at a particularly bemusing tennis match.

An snapped first. The whine in her voice betrayed her, she knew it, but it couldn't be helped. 'Well, I don't see what that's got to do with anything. You make her sound like some heroine of the diaspora. Mama Africa,' she sneered. 'Mummy knows what's going down between her and me. If she isn't prepared to take responsibility for her part in my childhood, I don't see why I should forgive and forget, just because it's convenient to do so. That's like asking me to be more mature than the parent.'

'Obviously totally impossible,' Dette said drily. She twisted in her seat, turning her back on An. 'But that's not what I see going on with you, Beth. You had a career, fashion design, glamorous! And your own place, independence. But you gave all that up to look after your Dad when he was sick. You helped your Mum. She told Ma she would've been lost without you, and now you're here, holding the fort while your Mum has a well earned rest. What is that if it's not duty?'

Beth poured herself a glass of vodka, hesitated then pushed it away from her. She buried her head in her hands and scratched her hairline with her fingertips. When she emerged her wrap was askew, and her face drawn. She gave An a look of infinite sadness. Holding her sister's gaze she said, as if to her alone, 'I don't know what to call it. Love, I suppose. At the end of the day, I was only given one mummy and one daddy. I had to make the most of them. Even if they didn't always make the most of me.'

12

Sex and Drugs and Rock'n'Roll

A biddly yeah, take it down.

Oh you're scatting, yeah you're singing, oh you really are The Swinging Moore Sisters. The coolest cats, the bathroom jazz band. Got the toothbrushes, smelling of Eggy Peggy sludge from the bottom of the toothmug. Got a strike on the sink. Now keep that beat; one, a-one, a-one two three four. Time to introduce Sister Beth on bass (also known as dental floss). Whoops, now she's on the laundry bin, that baddest of big drums. Take it away, Sis. Kicking. Going to take y'all into some freestyle now, hit the door, hit the bath, stamp your feet, swing that shower curtain. Really swing it. Sister Beth's switching like mad, she's alto, she's sax, you're taking the be bop dow woos, you're a wild scat cat, awroooo.

Come on, Big Sister. Need some help here. It's good, but it could be baaad! Let her fill in the gaps, let her do the harmonies. Where's the harm in it? Let her in . . . Yes! And now give a biiiig round of applause to Sister Margareta. Back from a long tour of the USA. Back by popular demand, please welcome a songstress to make your heart bleed . . . Greta, lead them on.

A rap rap rap. Not in the beat. Not a beat, a bang. Daddy's banging on the door, oh God. You're only playing. Improvised jazz, nothing's broken, promise. Only a bit of water on the floor and some Eggy Peggy on the windowsill. You can clean it up, he won't even notice. Dad, please, we haven't done anything.

But you ought to know better; after jazz come fairy tales and nursery rhymes: here's the big bad wolf. He'll huff and he'll puff and he'll blow your house down. Come out, ready or not. Counting: one, two, three. Then the Bells of London. Out the door with you. One arm, thick as a tree trunk across the gap. You've got to dodge down, under the arch. Run along now, little children. The belt's overhead, buckle end down and . . . Here comes a candle to light you to bed. All the way in, under the covers with you. No, Daddy, no, Daddy, no, Daddy . . . Here comes a chopper to chop . . . off . . . your . . . head.

With reluctance, An finally resorted to the stash of sleeping pills the hospital had prescribed. She hadn't needed them for a long time. Therapy helped her to stay on a level during the day; a kind of truce was achieved at night whereby the bad dreams stayed away as long as she looked after herself. This meant meditations, visualisations, plenty of fell walking and a healthy diet. She'd tried self medicating with alcohol, but that had nearly landed her back in hospital. Now it was an occasional treat.

Meanwhile, different, difficult circumstances prevailed. If she didn't get her sleep she would get threadbare, become unravelled. Sylvia, her therapist, had warned her that coming back to the homestead (and her father's death) would throw up new issues for her. Lead her down avenues as yet unexplored, perhaps as yet undiscovered. Not that she'd been trying to discourage An. In fact, she'd thought An had been ready for a while. Two years, she said, was a long time for someone as essentially healthy as An to avoid something so important. It was cheering to be pronounced 'essentially healthy'. So they had worked hard to prepare her. Only, An wished she had told Sylvia about seeing Steve.

For wasn't Steve the catalyst? Wasn't it her relationship with him that had led to that series of awful rows with Mummy and Daddy? To that final, fatal row that had heralded her breakdown and destroyed the only thing that gave her joy.

But she was better now. Bright and breezy, lemon squeezy. Summer in London, with her sister, with Steve. A whole three months with nothing to do but chill. Things would settle down with him, once they'd got used to being around each other again, once they had a proper talk. They still had strong feelings for each other; the rest would follow.

It was weird being in the homestead, but even that had changed. Seeing the kids hadn't been so terrible, in fact she and Dap had got on really well. Dap had given her her new address and said, 'Drop round any time, just give me a call first to say you're on your way.'

An sat up in bed and rubbed the sleep from her eyes. The thing about the pills was, you needed one hell of a kick start in the morning. The thought of immersing herself in a cold bath was not a happy one, but it gave her a gorgeous vital feeling afterwards. Look on the bright side, Anboleyn.

They took breakfast on the patio, in the shade of the house. An could see how Beth had put on weight so quickly. She

herself had fresh juice, grapefruit and a bowl of Greek yoghurt
while Beth had all of that and several croissants with jam.
But, looked at uncritically, Beth was a fine woman. Better for
the extra weight, if An was honest with herself. Yes she was
at least three dress sizes bigger, but that still made her only a
16 or 18 at most. Even if she were to get bigger, Beth could
carry it: she had a firm roundness around the hips and thighs,
a softness in the face and bosom; her skin, turning to burnt
umber in the exceptional heat, was taut, healthy. She was
beginning to develop a smudge of permanently dark skin
around her eyes, and often looked worryingly tired, but the
eyes themselves were as quick and bright as ever.

That morning Beth had combed out her hair, and it fell in
a heap of luscious black curls around her face. She had
Mummy's hair. What the older folks, in the old days, used to
call 'good hair'. Mummy always said her grandmother – their
great-grandma – was Indian, but when pressed was not able
to say what kind. From-India-Indian, or descended-from-
Arawak-Indian. It didn't matter, anyway. They soon learned
that half the African-Caribbeans they knew claimed to have
some 'Indian' ancestry. It seemed to confer some unfathom-
able prestige on them.

Whatever Indian there might have been had not worked
its way down the line to An. She was pure Nubian. People
often did not believe her when she said she was of Caribbean
parentage. She was ebony black, for one thing. And very tall
and thin with a high round backside. Her features were sharply
chiselled, her lips very full but firm and dark. She looked like
those pictures of Masai women they used to pore over in the
National Geographic, as children. The same hauteur, the calm,
erect pride.

In An's case it was only part natural. Their old music teacher, Mrs Farmer, had had stacks of the *National Geographic*. While one sister had her piano lesson the other would leaf through magazines, full of wonder for the other worlds revealed there. Apart from the starving Biafrans, these pictures of African tribes-people were some of the only images of black people they saw in those days. An studied the poses. Practised staring into the middle distance with her chin tilted just so, her face impassive. It suited her. Like her make-up, it was a good cover – a tribal mask.

Beth belched loudly and stretched her legs. 'Manners!'

'You sound just like Auntie.'

'God forbid.' Beth rubbed and patted her chest, emitting a series of short loud sighs. 'Yessir! Mmmm, hmmm. Yes!'

'You should be careful,' An laughed, 'it suits you.'

Beth grinned. She set about dusting the pastry crumbs off her dress. Suddenly An wanted to confess, to purchase some intimacy. 'I bought you some clothes, you know.'

'Oh yeah?' Beth looked up with interest. 'Where are they then? Let's have a shufti.'

'I wanted to give them to you when I got back, a kind of "good to see you" present. But last time I saw you, Beth, you were a mere slip of a girl. How was I to know? And then I was too embarrassed to tell you about them. And then I was vexed 'cos it made me look mean, not to have seen you for so long and not even brought you anything . . .' An trailed off, looking sheepish.

'Oh, you mean because I'm fat now?' Beth threw back her head and roared with laughter. 'Oh, Nita, you do get yourself in a tizz. I don't worry my pretty head about things like that. I feel so much more relaxed now I don't have to watch what

I'm eating. No more running to the bathroom scales after every meal. No more endless salads. You know, you should try it. Say yes to your universe. Say yes to chocolate cake.'

In the bedroom, An retrieved the kaftan and satin trousers from her suitcase and laid them out on the bed.

'Oh, that is *beautiful*.' Beth picked up the kaftan and held it to her face. She pored over the stitchwork and rubbed the fabric between her fingers.

'Tell you what,' she said, 'I can do something with this, add some extra panels here and here. Take the sleeves off and use them somewhere, let the back out a bit. You keep the trousers, they're more you anyway. Oh, thanks An. This is a perfect present.'

After that An felt so good she decided to phone Steve. She hadn't seen him since their first reunion, over a week ago. Obviously he was busy working, rescuing teenagers from the clutches of London. Or not. But it was the weekend soon, even a saint has a day of rest.

His voice was smooth and informal, as if he were answering the phone at home. It took a moment for him to realise who was on the other end. He offered no explanation or apology for not phoning her, as promised.

'Saturday, let me see. Oh, sorry babes, I'm on shift; double sleep-in. But midweek's good, let's say Wednesday. What do you want to do?'

There was no room for complaint, clearly she would just have to make the best of it. She tried not to let the disappointment tell in her voice. 'Maybe have a meal, see a film?'

'Nah, I'm booked in the evening.'

'But Steve, you just said . . .'

'Look, why don't we go to London Zoo. We can have lunch in Camden, have a look around the market and spend the rest of the afternoon at the Zoo. My treat. How does that sound?'

It made a change, at least, from Embankment Station.

Thriftiness is next to godliness. Money doesn't grow on trees, but if you look after the pennies, the pounds will look after themselves. Tomorrow is another day. Always put something aside for a rainy day, because Mother has, Father has, God bless the child that has its own.

Between them Mummy and Daddy had the whole patter on Money And The Importance Thereof, but it was Daddy who provided the object lesson. On the first Saturday of every month he sent one of the girls to the building society on the Broadway, to deposit his savings cheque. It was always a cheque, never cash – ready crossed and made over to Mr Moore, so it would be of no use to anybody if it were lost.

Great trust and responsibility were bestowed upon the carrier of the savings cheque and he expected it to be discharged with dignity and sobriety. Daddy knew that the second they were out of that front door the girls were liable to run amok, carrying on up and down the street, skinning up their teeth, making noise and generally making a show of themselves. That's why he never let them go together. It was a solitary task, so all the more a privilege.

The savings book had a soft cover in dark rose with gold and black lettering on the front. The cover was made of some strong, light material, halfway between paper and cloth. It didn't tear easily, but it was wearing at the edges. Black fingerprint smudges had etched their way into the crosshatch of textured lines that made up the fabric. They wouldn't yield to Mummy's efforts with a damp cloth. It became part of the ritual to wash your hands thoroughly in warm soapy water before 'the handing over of the book'.

Inside were a dozen pages of pale green paper. Each side of each sheet was marked out in columns and rows. Each row was numbered so you could calculate, at a glance, how many months you'd been saving for, multiply it by the sum of your savings cheque and cross check your calculation against the society's entry in the book. This was a nice bit of mental arithmetic to do when you got back from the Broadway. It was best to work it out on the way home because Daddy expected to get the answer as soon as he opened the front door. You couldn't just quote the figure lately entered in the credit column, in the building society's thin red ink. You had to show exactly how you'd arrived at your answer, plus interest and minus withdrawals, of course. Except that there never were any withdrawals.

Daddy saved a regular sum each month, varied every three years or so: first £8, then £12, then £20. It seemed a great deal to a child, compared to £1.00 a week pocket money, rising to £2.00 at age thirteen and ending abruptly with your first Saturday job, aged fourteen and a half. Although, as Daddy pointed out, he had to work outrageously hard for his money while the girls only had to act the fool. Taking turns to visit the BS (plus a dozen other lessons) would eventually cure them of all that.

The BS was housed in a bay-windowed shopfront, between the dry cleaner's and the chemist's. It was part estate agency, part solicitor's office, insurance brokerage and savings bank. It was locked in a time warp at around the 1950s. There were rarely any other customers. The wooden door was a peeling dirty white. In one window hung metal frames with photographs of homes for sale. They were never changed: they just got paler and paler. In the other window a dusty sign hung on a rusty chain. H. BAGSHOTT AND JOLLY. Nothing else, no clue as to their role, their function.

A sour-faced young man with unwashed hair served them. He scowled when the brass bell over the door announced the arrival of a customer. He snatched the book suspiciously from them as if they might have stolen it. He squinted at the cheque, left the bearer of the book standing in the middle of the carpet while he held a whispered conversation with a hidden colleague. Then he would reappear, and grudgingly enter a new figure in the book with a stuttering ink pen. He had to be Jolly. Bagshott (Helena, Hermione, Hildegarde?) was surely the plump, rosy cheeked motherly woman, who greeted them with a smile, offered them a seat, commented every single time that it was a nice tidy sum building up, whatever would their father do with all that money? And wiped her hands on her skirt if she accidentally touched them during the 'handing over of the book'.

There were two or three other people who crept around the BS, though none was memorable, and all completed the 'handing over of the book' with minimum fuss and minimum friendliness. Every one, though, seemed to share Daddy's reverence for money. This was embodied in the book. It was handed solemnly from person to person, deceptively slight but powerful beyond comprehension. Without money we are as dust.

Two things, then, were surprising to An. She considered them as she stroked on her mascara. The first thing, the one that really puzzled her, was that the old man had died intestate. It just didn't seem like a Daddy thing to do. You don't spend all your life going on and on about money and then make no provision for your hard-earned cash after you've gone. The second conundrum was that he had clearly been loaded.

An outlined her lips in burgundy and applied a first coat of lipstick. She totted up all the changes to the house: new double glazing and bathroom extension, completed the year before Daddy retired; all the downstairs rooms, except the extension, redecorated and/or refurbished the following year; plans to do upstairs this year or next.

Then there was the Caribbean cruise. And Beth's expensive new dress-making fabrics. Of course Beth might have had money of her own; she'd been in a reasonably well-paid job before she gave it up to play ministering angel. An pleated her lips and turned her head from side to side, considering. It didn't add up though. Beth had graduated at twenty-one after completing a four-year design degree in just three years. She had been at the homestead eight months, more or less, perhaps flitting between her own job and death duty for the first three months or so. That meant she'd have been earning for less than two years. Hardly time to amass a fortune.

It was just as well Steve was offering to pay for the zoo. With all this going out, and coming to the homestead instead of getting a holiday job this summer, she'd soon run out of dunzi. She took her make-up sponge and smoothed a little more foundation down her nose. She'd spent weeks and a small fortune tracking down this colour. It wasn't the most expensive – the one she'd bought before this one was the most expensive – but it was the nearest to her skin colour she could find. Dark as it was, it was not quite dark enough. An rubbed at the 'tide-mark' along her jawline, trying to blend the foundation.

That little old BS book had just been a teaching tool. The old man must have been stashing it away in some serious secret account all along. One thing rankled, but did not surprise her. She had none of the cash. No-one had mentioned money directly; all she knew was that there was no will, but Mummy had been to her solicitors and 'everything was sorted'. It appeared that Mummy, and by proxy, Beth, had it all.

13

Chicken George

'I'm pregnant.'

It's a whisper. She daren't say it out loud. She hadn't dared think it for weeks but she's getting wide now: her chest, always ample, billows into her armpits. There's an ache low in her pelvis, like the displaced memory of teeth growing. Baby growing. In there. Beth rests her hands on the rising dome of her belly.

'I'm pregnant.'

She can't believe her own goofy grin in the mirror. They've got no money. She's doing A levels in the summer, he's still at tec. And their parents will flip. What the hell has she got to smile about? Baby growing. His baby. She throws back her head and laughs.

Outside the bathroom door, An's waiting. For a moment there's a flicker of Greta – watchful, suspicious – then it's only An again, just turned sweet seventeen, happier than she's ever been.

'You talking to yourself? First sign of madness!'

If Beth told her, told her sister, they could laugh together. Share the joy . . . maybe . . .

'Oh, shut up. Get out the way or I'll be late for school.'

Later she leaps about the bedroom, trying it out. Now she's herself: 'I'm pregnant.' She bounces to the other bed, playing An. 'Oh, Beth, congratulations, I'm so happy for you. George will make a wonderful father. When's the big day?'

They'll get married first, of course. They'll have to be quick; already you can see the bump if you know what to look for. And get their names down for a council flat. Then there'll be things to buy, baby clothes and bits, all the tiny vests and bootees. Bonnets for a winter baby. Mummy won't like it at first but she'll come round. For god's sake, she had two children before exchanging any vows. Anyway, she'll just love being a grandmother. Maybe Mummy will let her have the cot from out the loft. Would they let a married woman stay at school? Daddy'd know.

She can't help it, she just *has* to tell someone. She's knocking at her sister's bedroom door before she can think twice.

'An, I've got a secret. You're the first to know.'

Tall and nappy-headed, grey skin bwoy. Soft on the outside. Soft on the inside. He walked with a lollop and his head cocked to one side. Mummy said it was because Mrs Goode had knocked all the sense and stuffing out of him. She beat that child. Lord, she really beat that child. Sometimes, when they were lying up in his bed after school – in the precious hour before Mrs Goode came home from the Co-op – Beth would stroke her fingers in the air above his scars and wince for him.

It was like they were the same person. Everything was understood. They never talked about each other's parents, other than to say: 'I've got to get back, they'll be wondering where I am.' Or: 'We can go out Saturday, she's working till six.'

At school he sat behind her in lessons, trying not to think about kissing her neck. Laughing to himself as she stroked the very inch of skin he'd been thinking about. Otherwise they avoided each other, passing in the playground with averted eyes. It was a pact they'd made. Studies were everything, the only way out. It was easier when he left for technical college; they could concentrate without the pull of the other's proximity. He'd get a good job – as an engineer or a computer programmer. She'd go on to university. They'd move away, buy a little house, have children, look to the future. Nothing that happened now mattered. Soon they'd be free of it all.

They were seventeen the first time they slept together. Mrs Goode had gone up to Birmingham because her only sister had died. Etta Goode had left behind three orphaned children and a four-storey tenanted house. It was a whole heap of paperwork to sort out. A week stretched into a month, a month into a summer.

The very first day was a Saturday. Beth left the house in her royal blue uniform and sensible shoes. She walked down Texas Street, into Fallow Lane and stopped at the phone box on the corner. She could see the shopping centre as she dialled; imagined her supervisor in one of the offices behind the concrete facade, peering out into the car park as she commiserated with Beth and hoped her period pain eased up soon.

George was waiting in the hallway, his mouth spread so wide she thought his face would split. The tears welled up in her eyes.

'I'm sorry you had to lie, Betty. I know you hate it.'

Actually, after three years of it, lying had become second nature. That wasn't the problem at all.

'I didn't have to lie. I really am on.' She hung her head and sobbed. George just stood there, looking at her.

She was about to wipe her tears and go home when he took her hand. 'Come.'

He led her upstairs and into the bathroom. He took her bag from her shoulder and emptied the contents onto the lino. He squatted down and considered them, prodding her Tampax with a finger like an Aborigine reading tracks.

'George?'

'Ssh. Sssh, darling.'

He stood and began to undress her.

'Take it out,' he said, and ushered her towards the toilet. Then he helped her into the bath. Gently, he soaped her, showered her down, helped her out again and patted her dry as if she were a small, fragile child. He left the towel draped around her shoulders. Beth stood on the bathmat and watched him. She felt very calm. He handed her a fresh tampon and she put it in. Then he wiped her between her legs again with a damp flannel.

'Come.'

Beth put her hand in his and followed him into his bedroom. She sat on the bed while he undressed. Their eyes never left each other's faces. When he was naked also, George knelt at her feet. Only then did they let their gaze wander; their faces glowed with astonishment. He put his hands on her thighs. For the first time since they had climbed the stairs, she felt nervous.

'George, are you sure?'

'Betty, I love you,' he said. And kissed her.

If she was a tree, she'd be a rubber tree: his tongue left fissures in her skin, from her knees to her thighs. And she could swear she could feel the sap rising, thick and sweet, gathering inside her and endlessly flowing out. He was drinking her, line after line of her, moving up her body with his lapping tongue. Beth's fingers, reading his back, found the same lines in him; little ridges of scar tissue and underneath the ripple of his muscles.

If he was a river he'd be the Nile. Trickling from a dozen tiny tributaries, all the parts of him, slowly at first then with growing urgency, with sureness. Everything that he was had found a purpose. The strands of him met and knit, and rushed on. He was a bright right wide river, she was his source. It wasn't his first time; he knew it was hers. And he knew that with Beth he had gone back to the beginning.

After he had loved her with his mouth he loved her with his hands. It was terrible, the urge to climb into his skin, to have him so deep inside her she *was* him. Beth lay on the bed, crooning. Her body did things of its own volition; rippled and shivered and jumped. Beside her George curled and uncurled, curled and uncurled. He was like one of those tiny hairless caterpillars that hang on the underside of leaves, his whole body a sensor. Curling. Uncurling.

He began to cry. 'Ah, Betty, I need . . . please, I can't, I have to . . .'

She was going to burst, they were both going to. The bits would fly about the room and stick to things. Everything splattered on the walls. The blood and the come. When Mrs Goode came home she'd think there'd been a murder and she'd never guess what had really gone on. Never guess the pleasure that had gone into this spectacular death . . . Christ, what was she thinking of? She was going mad. Beth sprang off the bed and ran.

Just as she got back, he started to uncurl again. She paused for a moment beside the bed, watching him open – beautiful flower, his head and limbs the petals. His stamen quivered, sending out vibrations. She bent her head and kissed up the droplets gathering there; sweet as honey for the bee. George opened his eyes and looked at her. The tears sat in his lashes like dew. She could feel the effort it took him not to thrust himself into her mouth. It was time. He sat up to meet her as she climbed into his lap. Their sigh was a butterfly, taking wing. Flying over the river, over the delta and out to the open sea.

A man's gotta do what a man's gotta do. Never shirk from his duty, let his courage be the measure of him. Man must provide for his woman, his son, do whatever it takes.

Beth had to admit she was tickled; she'd laughed when she first heard about it. Her hero. At school all the littler kids took the role of George in the playground. His unique lollop became a swagger; his tipsy head the under-the-eyebrows stare of a man on a mission. When someone brought in a hot-off-the-press edition of the *Hendon Times*, she'd laughed again.

LOCAL BOY, GEORGE, HOLDS UP 'CHICKEN KITCHEN' WITH REPLICA SAWN-OFF SHOTGUN.

Of course; why hadn't she seen it before? Chicken George! Beth and her friends laughed so hard they slid off their chairs and rolled around on the floor. Chicken George, the robber baron of West Hendon. Demanding all the money in the till, plus a family size bucket and a litre of coke. The girls sang to the tune of the old reggae hit. *Eighteen with a drumstick; got a finger on the wishbone, gonna pull it.* Underneath, though, Beth was prouder than she could ever say. Fancy George doing all that for her?

The baby had messed up their plans. Not that they regretted it for a moment. It only meant they'd be together sooner, their new, adult life would begin almost at once instead of in three years' time. Beth was ready to adapt. After the initial shock of finding herself pregnant, she had realised that everything she wanted she already had.

George was worried, though. Beth would tire of a council flat at the scruffy end of the borough. She'd regret her lost university career, her lost ambitions. And his mother: what would she say? That he was wut'less, a failure. She'd struggled all these years to raise him right. Damn near broke his back beating out the wastrel in him that was his father and now . . . The only way to salvage the situation was to get some money, fast. Money was always the answer.

Arrest and a caution, Beth thought. It was only a replica gun and anyway, George wasn't a very good robber. He'd got away with the grand sum of eighty-two pounds and thirty-six pence. And had been apprehended within two streets of the crime scene – a blow-out on his bike landing him in the gutter with a sprained ankle. Daft sod.

She stopped laughing during the court hearing. Mrs Goode sat two rows from the dock, weeping. Her face was shiny with tears, the skin stretched and hot looking. The shame rose off her in waves. George was remanded on bail, pending social-enquiry reports. Mrs Goode had to stand and confirm that she was prepared to have him at home during this time. Her hands shook; her mouth shook; her voice was a mere whisper and she was asked to speak up. 'Yes, your honour,' with the emphasis on the 'h'. No youth custody places were available. The alternative would have been prison but he'd probably end up there anyway. After the hearing she passed Beth in the corridor and hissed at her: 'See what you've brought my only child to? God going to take that bastard you have in there and then you will see what crosses I have to bear.'

Ruination and despair. Everything broken, finished. You follow the straight and narrow path or you find yourself up Shit Creek. Beth was stupid to think it could ever have been otherwise.

14

The Franklins

Dozing in the garden. An struggled to uncurl herself, feeling the tension build along her spine. She often woke like that, like a fossil from the seabed: coiled ammonite or the opposite, splayed starfish. The pain was starting in her leg, grating through the muscle. She rolled onto her back and breathed deeply. She must orient herself, visualise her space. Eyes still closed against the sun's glare. An 'walked' herself around the garden.

Here was the wall of the extension, brick hot under her hand. The two picture windows hid the interior with a froth of net curtain. The double doors were flung open to the heat. Here was the yellow and red patio, fading year by year, reverting to grey cement. Here was the garden path. The black barley twist border tiles stuck up like tipsy gravestones, all the way along the edge of the lawn. Following the path, she passed the flower beds, brimming with foliage she'd never learned the names of. She came to the raised bed at the end of the garden. To the butchered apple tree and the shed that used to cower in its shade. Now it paled in the bleaching sun. Like the fence that ran along two sides of the garden, it was turning to tinder.

Turning, she crossed the lawn. The grass was still springy underfoot – thanks to Beth's loving care – but the edges had begun to burn. Finally she came to the remaining apple tree. This one was young and healthy though tending to twist a little. It gave a dappled shade, harbouring oases of cool against the swelter of the garden in the afternoon. The tree bore fruit, promising an abundance this year. Underneath the apple tree was An, flopped on an assortment of blankets, belly up in the sun.

She raised her knees, folded her arms under her head and stretched, arching her back until her breasts threatened to break loose. She observed them now, taut orbs metallic with the sheen of sweat like a pair of boules rolling gently in the thin cotton of her blouse. It made her randy: the sun, the sight of herself, the day spinning away into oblivion. Those lazy hazy crazy days of summer were back again.

An smiled and wriggled her hips. The heat was beating through the fabric of her shorts. It was lovely, like being licked by a warm wet tongue. Or feeling the press of a sweaty palm . . . Steve's voice whispered in her ear, 'Turn over,' and she rolled onto her stomach. The heat between her legs stayed, began to spread over her buttocks, her back. A puff of cool air tickled her hair. She could feel her breasts, crushed into the baked earth. She moved her arms out to accommodate them, lay with her cheek to the blanket, a long blade of grass waving under her nose.

Steve would straddle her, sitting lightly just below her shoulders so his balls rested in the curve of her back. He'd stroke the inside of her legs, from the ankle up, pausing to lick her calves, biting and squeezing the firm flesh. He could make an orifice out of anything: the crook of her arm, her armpit, the crease behind her ear, the backs of her knees. He would dally at each one, teasing her till she thrashed like a landed fish. He would stand, leave her suddenly cold and panting at his feet, straining her neck to see him, his face disappearing into the high distance, a god with his head in the clouds.

Then he would kneel, behind her; he would use his thighs to press hers apart. And his hands to hold her open. Just the tips of his fingers touching her, sliding in the edge of her wet. That was all. The air and heat would do his work for him. When she began to mewl and rear, when she clawed the ground, incoherent with want . . . Roughly, his hands would grip her hips. He'd pull her to him and enter her in one long smooth exquisite movement. And again and again until her toes her neck her nipples her stomach, every part of her clenched and pulsed and opened. Until she was explosion and implosion. Sweat and saliva running off her face. Forcing herself back and back on him. Until she dropped on the bed, wrung out in his grasp. Until she writhed and rose again, keening, screaming.

An bit on her knuckles till her teeth ached. She scrambled up, praying she could make it to her room without meeting Beth. She'd never had it so good.

'We'll start in the middle and work our way out to the edges. I'll have the speckled brush, you can have the kettle. Fair trade?'

An nodded, it was all one to her, which brush, which portion of creosote. She hitched up her overalls and bent her head to the treacly liquid rippling in the paint kettle. It was a shock, the smell so sharp it made her gasp. Blowing, laughing, wrinkling her nose, she stood and finished tying the scarf around her hair. Beth waited by the fence, wearing Daddy's black plastic apron. She had gone to outlandish lengths to preserve her good looks. Her hair was capped in a stocking top and swaddled in a length of old bandage. She had her sunglasses on and had smeared her face with Vaseline to protect against stray splashes. She looked like an outsized mutant beetle. An hid a smile and joined her sister on the flower bed.

'Now, be really careful. We're trampling things as it is.'

They braced their legs, dipped their brushes; 'Ready, steady, GO!'

It took three times as long and was ten times as hard as it looked. The wood drank creosote by the slavering black brush load: belched, bubbled and paled again as if it had never been touched. They worked their way up and down the flower bed, finding the starting point already dry by the time they returned to it. They left a path of crushed petals in their wake. The bunched roses were dropping and bruised where they had brushed past them repeatedly. The scent released was no match for the pungent stench of creosote. By late afternoon they were done, and done in.

Beth sat on the grass and pulled off her bandage turban. Underneath, the little nylon skullcap formed from the stocking top had pressed a deep ridge around her head. She peeled this off too and shook out her curls. Pressing her fingertips into the angry red welt she sighed, staring through the moving cradle of her fingers at the fence.

'Never again. Next time we'll get a man in.'

'Next time?' An, stripping frantically down to her underwear, paused. Her T-shirt was half-way over her head, her
arms sticking in the air like a puppet's.

'It needs doing every year, really. Then it's not so bad. Even
so, that is not an experience I'm keen to repeat. An, for God's
sake, the neighbours!'

'So you'll be here for a while, then.' An re-arranged the
T-shirt and sat beside her sister to inch her overalls off over
her trainers. 'I thought, now that Daddy's . . . when Mummy
comes . . .'

'I haven't decided. In any case, I'll still be nearby, and she'll
still need help. It's a lot of work, keeping up a house like this.'

An nodded, feeling suddenly, searingly jealous.

'And you? Will you be here when Mummy gets back or
were you planning to avoid her for the rest of your life?'

'What's the point, Beth?'

'What do you mean, "what's the point?"'

'We only fight. Is that what you want? The way it used to
be, with her screaming and me crying?'

'I think it was the other way round. Anyway,' Beth reached
out a tar-stained hand and cupped her sister under the chin.
'Things are different now. Surely you can try? Just a little, for
me?'

An dropped her lashes, refusing to meet Beth's gaze. She
took the hand, held it, placed it on the grass and patted it
gently. She wrapped her arms around her knees. 'Is that what
she wants?'

'She doesn't understand why you seem so angry. She says
she knows things were tough sometimes, when we were
growing up, and she wasn't always fair. But she did her best,
really she did. And at the end of the day Daddy was the boss.

You know that; there was no difference between her and us most of the time. You can't keep . . .'

'Mummy's just a cloth monkey. We both used to know that, Beth. Then you started acting like she was real. Maybe she was for you. Maybe all you needed was soft fur, a teat for milk, the *look* of a mummy.'

Beth took a deep breath and narrowed her eyes. 'You see, An, this is why you get on my nerves.'

A flash of heat swept through An's chest again. She jutted her chin out belligerently. 'Why? Because I'm not afraid of the truth?'

'You wouldn't know the truth if it jumped up and slapped you. You've spent your whole life on frigging fantasy island.'

An started to speak quickly, the words tumbling over each other in their haste to get out of her mouth. 'It was you, you told me about it. You came home from school one day; sociology. You couldn't believe it. You had the book right there and we looked at it together. It was some kind of behavioural experiment in the fifties. They took these baby monkeys and they left one group with their mother. Then they made some false mummies out of wire and put a teat in for feeding, only they covered one with fur, real monkey fur. And they watched to see how they grew. I mean, Christ, it's so obvious, so cruel. Beth, there's no way you could forget something like that.'

Beth was quiet for a long time. She put her hands over her face.

'What happened then?'

'The babies that grew with their monkey mummy, they were fine. The ones with just the wire monkey: well, they fought each other and banged their heads on the cages and rocked themselves and suffered. They even tried to harm themselves and some of them died. Just from sadness.' She was almost whispering. 'And when they had babies of their own they killed them.'

Beth lurched over in the grass and tried to get up. 'That's it; enough. You say one more word and I swear I'll . . .'

'For God's sake, Beth, that wasn't us. You should *know* this. There was a third group, remember? The ones with the cloth monkey. Yes, they fought too and they cried out in distress. But most of them were alright. When they had their own babies they tried to cuddle them. They weren't always very good at it but they tried to mother them. That's us, Beth; the children of the cloth monkey.'

When her sister finally spoke her voice was muffled. 'Is that all?'

'You'll get another chance, you know. There'll be other babies.'

'I don't want to have this conversation right now.'

'You started it, remember.'

'Yeah, well.' Beth rubbed her face with the heel of her hand, leaving a smear of creosote under her eyes.

An jumped up and strode towards the house. Her overalls trailed behind her like a limp tail. 'I'm going for a shower. Then I thought I'd take a walk, have a look at the Franklins' house.'

Beth looked up. An stood on the patio, grinning at her, wolfish in the shadows. Then she turned and disappeared into the gloom.

'That's the Franklins', the one with the red door.'

'Isn't it the black door? Remember, we liked the busy lizzie in the porch window?'

'No, it's the red – number 20. I should know, they're my friends.'

'Alright, the red door then. But they're my friends too.'

'Let's stop and look. The path's nice, isn't it, all those coloured tiles? And the door with the patterns on the glass, and the red shiny paint matching the red roses in the stained glass at the top where the number 20 is.'

'Don't, Ni, if they see you leaning on the gate they might come out.'

'It doesn't matter. It will only be Mr Franklin. He'll only say "hello girls". He might ask us in for breakfast.'

'We've already had breakfast. Anyway, we'll be late for school, come on.'

'Mr Franklin . . .'

'Wait! There's a car coming. Alright, cross now.'

'Mr Franklin is an armchair dad, like all English dads. He sits in his armchair all weekend.'

'Daddy sits in an armchair.'

'No, but it's not the same. Armchair dads are different. They sit and smile and let the mums run things.'

'Mr Franklin says, "Can we have some more tea, please, Mother?"'

'And Mrs Franklin calls him Dad, like she's just Jackie's age, and she . . .'

'Which one is Jackie?'

'The youngest one, the one with the long black hair in a plait.'

'It's blonde!'

'No it's not, it's black. They've all got black hair, and blue eyes, you don't remember anything. Anyway, I was saying, Mrs Franklin sits on Dad Franklin's knee and kisses his nose.

Your turn now, but Li, you've got to stick to the rules or it's no good. You can't change things.'

'Alright then. Let's see. Mrs Franklin cooks bangers for dinner every night. With spaghetti hoops and a fried egg. Sometimes the sausages burst, and pink meat comes out and kind of goes frothy, and by the time the skin is crispy the bit that's come out has gone black. Inside they're still pink and they melt in your mouth, and you can have three . . .'

'Or four!'

'Or five if you want. And chips.'

'Mr Franklin says, "Pass the sauce, please, Mother," and he winks at Jackie and Frances and Sandra and Peter, and he ruffles Peter's curly hair. He picks up his sausages with his fingers, and he takes a big bite and takes it out of his mouth and drops it on the floor for the dog when Mother Franklin's not looking.'

'But she does know, and she doesn't mind.'

'After tea Mr Franklin says "Righto" and claps his hands. He says, "homework", and looks at them with his serious face. And they go upstairs feeling a bit sad because he's not usually strict . . .'

'And as soon as they get to the top he claps his hands again and says, "*Grange Hill* in half an hour. Last one down's a wally."'

'A wally. I like that. Li, let's go up this way and into Vivien Avenue.'

'No, the Boroughs is quicker. Whose turn is it?'

'Mine. Mr Franklin's not very very clever . . .'

'He's not stupid.'

'No, he knows just enough to help the children with their homework, and to explain things so that even Jackie and Peter understand.'

'He never says "Go and fetch the Pendlebury." Stupid maths book, so old the cover's gone black like a falling off scab, and it says "thou" and "hence" and things in Latin.'

'Scabby Pendlebury.'

'Mr Franklin never sits behind you in his chair while you do maths out of the Pendlebury, with his spare belt over the arm, waiting for you to make a mistake. And he never laughs when Jackie can't get her words out.'

'Because Jackie can always get her words out. Mr Franklin is the children's friend.'

'And Mrs Franklin. Every night they take turns to read the children a story in bed. Even Sandra, who's twelve the same as me, and pretends she's too big for stories in bed. Mrs Franklin says, "You're never too old to be a child" . . .'

'And she tucks them all up in bed. And Mr and Mrs Franklin say, "Night night now, children. God bless, we love you." They never forget, every single night.'

'But even if they didn't say it, even if they forgot to say it for a hundred nights, the children wouldn't mind. Because they know it anyway.'

15

London Zoo

The population of Camden Town doubles, even trebles on a hot day. After a series of scorchers the place resembled an African market. Goods were laid out on brightly coloured blankets on the pavement or in battered suitcases propped up on orange crates. Music blared from a dozen stalls and shop PAs. Huge bundles of phallic incense sticks wafted their hot musk into the dusty air. Rakish young men, decked out in daishikis, resplendent in the Colours, hawked armloads of twine bracelets; black for the colour of our skin, red for the colour of our blood . . . Japanese students in outlandish shoes propped themselves against the railings, the throaty timbre of a Peruvian flute weaving its way amongst them.

Assorted tables and rickety chairs appeared up and down the pavement, some with precarious looking umbrellas balanced on top of them. Sandwich boards advertising ice-cold drinks and slices-o-pizza tripped those foolish enough to think that pavements were for walking on. Most people took to the roads, veering out from the gutter in unpredictable swarms. It drove the drivers mad. Camden Town underground stands at the apex of two main roads. Even from inside the station, the noise of car horns was deafening.

An trotted up the escalator as fast as she could. Her progress was hampered by tourists and chilled-out Londoners for whom it was too hot to observe the laws of the moving staircase. 'Stand to the right, walk up the left. Stand to the right, God, what's the matter with you people?'

An muttered and shoved her way to the top, earning laughter and blank looks as she went. Steve was waiting on the other side of the ticket barrier. He grabbed her arm and together they tunnelled out onto Kentish Town Road.

'Jeez! There's going to be a nasty accident down there today if they're not careful, it's heaving. I'm melting.'

They stopped while An rummaged in her rucksack for her washbag. She always carried a damp flannel on days like this, a little bottle of mineral water and some sachets of 4–7–11 wet-wipes. Turning aside from Steve she mopped her face and neck, dipping her hand inside her basque to freshen her cleavage. She rubbed cologne over her palms and inner thighs, as far as her shorts would allow. Then she felt human again.

'Finished in the bathroom, have we?' Steve looked her up and down, arms folded. 'I mean, don't mind me and all these strangers. Just go right ahead.'

An wrinkled her nose. 'No-one's looking. Really, Steve, it's not like you to be so prudish.' She put her arm through his again. 'I seem to remember you liked doing private things in public.'

Very gently, he disengaged himself. 'Too hot for that.'

They continued along Kentish Town Road, avoiding the crush. A new cafe had opened up across the road. Its facade was almost all glass and through it An glimpsed a cavernous interior, done out in earth reds and midnight blue, with indiscernible shapes swinging from the ceiling in the breeze of a giant fan. It was clearly the haunt of fashionable twenty-somethings, insouciant in the shadows, watching the world go by. A few tourists crowded around the two token tables set out on the pavement but the road had little to offer them and they got up to leave as An and Steve approached. An wondered if they would have lunch there but Steve seemed to have other ideas. He marched resolutely past and, placing his hand lightly in the small of her back, steered her back onto the thoroughfare.

'I thought we might take a boat trip,' he spoke close to her ear. Beside them a monster ghettoblaster was being carried aloft on the bare sunburned shoulder of a dreadlocked wanna-be. Steve put his arm round her waist and drew her to him. His breath whispered through the fine hairs on the side of her face. 'Up to Regent's Park. It'll be nice and cool. The next boat's at quarter to.'

An glanced at her watch. Just gone twelve, barely time for lunch. As she turned to say it, Steve brushed her cheek with his lips.

They contented themselves with an apple each and half a Crunchie bar, courtesy of An's capacious rucksack, and joined the queue for the river trip. It was a popular choice, and they only just got on. Down by the canal the air was fresher. As the boat pushed out from the jetty and executed a laborious turn, An shivered and stretched out her hands to receive the breeze.

It is funny, how you can be born and bred in a place and never do the things that other people come from halfway round the world to do. But it wasn't quite as she imagined it.

For a start the boat was battered and small; no cafe, no down-stairs or deck, nothing to buy on board. A man in a torn striped T-shirt swung himself around a pole and clambered over the canopy, straightening things, in between giving them a potted history of the route.

As they chugged along, An wished she'd brought her camera. The barges moored on either side were decked out with hanging baskets, tropical pot plants and colourful painted signs. Everything was pristine, on display. She found herself thinking, Mummy would love this. Mummy would say, 'Phew! look at that,' and whistle between her teeth. She would call out to the inhabitants of the barges and beg them for a cutting, 'just a small one, just throw it down. You know, they grow to ten times the size in Jamaica.' Mummy's delight in the flowers, in the quaint barges, in the incredibly fat ginger cat that lounged on a sundeck, would be smug, knowing. As if she herself had some part to play in this perfection. Nah, An was glad she didn't have her camera. Taking pictures would be such a Mummy thing to do. The eternal, eternally embarrass-ing tourist.

Near the end of their journey they passed through a long tunnel. Striped T-shirt explained that, before the advent of the engine, small children would be used to push the barges through, bracing their backs against the barge and their feet against the damp mossy walls of the tunnel. Foot over foot till the boat was out the other side. It probably took well over an hour. A thrilled gasp went up amongst the passengers.

As they disembarked Steve said loudly, 'That's nothing. This lot should take a stroll under the Arches one afternoon, have a look round Cardboard City. Then they'd know about Victorian expediency.'

Zoos were really depressing, they agreed. They watched the monkeys scoot around their cage in a short series of hysterical runs. Over the tyre, down the pole, diagonally across the bottom then up the side. Next time, through the tyre, zig-zag the fence, under the branch, spiral the pole. Now, swing on the tyre, hop off the fence, jump down to the ground . . . One of them kept showing its bottom; another made faces at the sky at exactly ten-second intervals. An felt sickened. All the same, she would have liked to check out the seals' display at two o'clock.

Instead, they left the zoo and went into Regent's Park. They bought chips and soft drinks at the canteen and stretched out on the scorched grass to eat. The park was crowded. Steve found them a spot on the very boundary, under the miserly shade of a hedge.

He lay on his stomach, popping hot chips into his mouth and doodling on a scrap of paper. An leaned over for a shufti. Hearts and flowers, one smiley face, another sad, with a single tear. In the centre of the masterpiece Steve had scrawled the word Evian, like the water. As she watched he wrote it out again and again, in different scripts. Bubble letters, italics, capitals. This time he split the word: 'Evi' 'An'.

An smiled and sat back, arms wrapped loosely around her knees. It was like the name trail game she used to play as a child. Evi-An was a good one. Stevie was a sweetie.

'We should come up here with a proper picnic next time,' she said eyeing a couple under a nearby tree, slowly bringing extravagant items out of a hamper.

'Nah. You'd get fat with all those strawberries and cream and ting-and-ting.'

'Ting-and-ting? Ting-and-ting!' An roared. 'Stevie, you've

been hanging round with black folks. Eh, eh. Next thing it'll be I-and-I, Raaaastafari. Don't do it. Your Mum wouldn't like the hairstyle.'

The notion of Steve in a knitted tam, waving dusty brown dreadlocks, looking like Locksman Eddie, tickled her so much she rolled around on the grass, clutching her stomach. Steve lay beside her, propped up on one elbow, grinning. He laughed, 'Heh, heh,' and it set her off again.

Quietening, An sat up and wiped her tears away. 'Oh, you're precious, you are. Ting-and-ting!'

'Come here.'

He reached out and pulled her against him. Her bare legs grazed across the stubbly straw of the lawn. An opened her mouth to protest and he kissed her, roughly. He put one hand in her hair and held onto the curls. He pushed his pelvis at her and groaned.

'God, I wanna fuck you. Right here. Now.'

'Steve, you're hurting me.'

'Like this, mmmm? And this?' He buried his mouth against her neck and sucked fiercely. He took his hand out of her hair and jammed it onto her breast.

'No!' An struggled away from him and sat up. She wiped his spittle off her neck with a quick angry movement, then hugged her knees and stared into the distance. Beside her, she heard Steve panting. She watched out of the corner of her eye as he straightened his clothes and put a hand between his legs, trying to shift his erection. Then he too sat up. 'Private things in public, remember?'

An stared resolutely ahead. The couple with the hamper were whispering to one another. The woman glanced over her shoulder at them and immediately away again. Nearby, a woman who had been descending the slope towards them called to her children.

'Betsy, Garth. Come away. No, you can't watch the people fighting. Come here now.'

An felt completely humiliated. Everyone must have seen. They probably thought she was a prostitute or something. She knew Steve liked to be daring, thought that nearly being caught gave proceedings an extra frisson. A grope in the cinema; down not so dark alleyways. Once, memorably, at the bottom of some steps with the Thames lapping at their feet. They'd come a cropper then. She'd slipped, with her knickers round her ankles, and brought him crashing down on top of her. They both had to go home by taxi, soaking wet and covered with river slime. But this was too much. It was broad daylight. On the other side of the hedge, red double decker buses rumbled past. All the passengers on the top deck, they must have seen them, twisting around on the grass like something out of *Ai No Corrida*.

Steve put a hand on her bare back and began to knead gently at the base of her neck. An stretched and sighed. She was trembling. She was getting wet. Suddenly, Steve jumped up and pulled her to her feet. He picked up An's rucksack and thrust it into her arms. They stared at each other for a moment, breathing noisily.

'Come on,' Steve muttered, 'I know a hotel nearby.'

16

The Music Man

The house is winding down, it's nearly bedtime. Mummy in the kitchen, Beth in our room, Daddy in his palace. You don't know why it's Daddy's palace. Mummy chose the furniture and does all the dusting and hoovering. It just is. Only he is allowed to use it every day. He can mess it up if he wants to, cover it with papers and books, push the coffee table into the corner. Put his cigars out in the planter and leave the stubs there, hidden by the thick shiny leaves of the rubber plant, for Mummy to find and tut over. She never tells him off, though. Ever. After all, his money paid for it. For the room and the planter. For the cigars and even the rubber plant. His money pays for everything. So he can do just as he pleases.

It pleases him for you to know all this, and you show it in the little ways he has taught you. Tonight you're bringing cigars. They live in a flat box of pale rough wood with some pictures painted on the lid that have faded so you can't see what they are anymore. The box is very old. Inside is lined with soft red cloth pinched into little channels where the cigars lie, snug as babies. On Saturdays you take it in turns to go to the newspaper shop and buy a packet of Hamlet, wrapped in cardboard and cellophane. For a treat Daddy lets you unwrap the new box, crinkling up the cellophane to throw in the fire. Then you take out the cigars, one by one, and carefully tuck them in their red nests till the box is full.

You stretch up as tall as you can and reach into the top drawer of the tallboy. In amongst Daddy's socks and his brown and beige check handkerchiefs is the cigar box. The drawer smells of aftershave and smoking. Of Daddies and safety. You close it carefully and walk out of the bedroom, balancing the box on your palms.

It's dark in the room and in the hallway. Mummy hasn't turned the lights on yet. She says everyone has to conserve electricity, it costs a lot of money. She says you can see perfectly well until about eight o'clock, and even then you don't need all the lights burning. Back home they use oil lamps. They give a lovely light, she says. Perhaps we should get some. But Daddy says it's not modern, and we're in England now.

As you go down the stairs you slide your feet so you know where the old step ends and the new one begins. You have to keep your eyes down, on the box and on the shadows of your feet peeping out below. If the light was on you could lift up your head and it would be like a ceremonial dance, a procession. You can hear Daddy playing the Bolero and you go downstairs and into the front room in time to the music.

Daddy is in his chair by the window. His feet are up on the coffee table. He nods when he sees you, but he doesn't stop conducting the music, sweeping up and down with both hands.

'Boom, da, da!' he says. 'Boom!'

You put the cigars down on the edge of the table nearest to him. You wait, hands folded in front of you. He doesn't tell you to leave so you sit down, making yourself as tiny as possible in the settee.

This is the best bit, where the elephants come in. They sway from side to side and wave their trunks. Their feet are like thunder on the sun-baked earth. On their heads they have red silk squares, edged with tassels. Diamond earrings in their ears, gold tips on their tusks. The elephants lift up their trunks and trumpet.

'Boom! Boom!'

Daddy lifts his head and the light shimmers on his glasses so his eyes are just circles of yellow like twin suns. He grins at you and you grin back, like a Cheshire cat, like he usually tells you not to, skinning up your teeth. The music is shaking you, filling the room. Cacophonous. You looked it up in the dictionary. The music is cacophonous, but it's beautiful too, wheezing and shouting, then high pitched and low. It's louder and louder. *This* is the best bit. Daddy jumps to his feet and throws up his arms. He opens his mouth but you can't tell if he's making any noise. He's like a hero, a film star, standing at the gates of his palace commanding the crowds and the elephants, accepting the roar of his people.

And you are his favourite and he lets you watch.

She stood in the warm evening air, composing herself. Passed a self-conscious hand over her bare collar bone, pulled down her shorts at the back, straightened her belt. Beth had such a sharp eye, almost a sixth sense sometimes, she'd notice if anything were amiss. Clothes awry, make-up bruised.

An was in no mood to have to justify herself. It was just gone ten o'clock. Perfectly feasible that she and Steve had spent the day out and gone for a meal and a drink. Instead of signing Mr and Mrs Moore in the stained register of a cheap hotel, her eyes sliding away from the gaze – contemptuous, mocking, bored? – of the teenage receptionist.

They had fumbled their way up the stairs, their fingers locked in each other's clothing, banging their mouths together, burning themselves on the carpet. Inside the room they tumbled into a wriggled heap of limbs and wet things; lips and tongues and genitals, not bothering to switch on the light, or undress. They had found apertures in each other's clothing, sucked and licked through these. Snuffled, chewed, explored with their fingers, the wet cloth snagging, rubbing against skin.

Musty carpet tickled her nose. Her face rested on something small and soft. Fluff ball? Dead mouse? An twisted her head and located the shadowy bulk of the bed, rising out of the gloom like a ship in fog. Dragging Steve after her, his mouth still attached, An wrestled them up and onto the duvet. Where, finally, they undressed, fucked, and she cried out in an ecstasy of disappointment.

It was slipping away from her, as it always did. The burn and the urge. Heat and need, trickling wet. The hope that this time, this time. She arched her back and bounced him off her pelvis, thrusting at him, go on, go on, go on. She crossed her ankles over his buttocks to push him further. Trying to feel something. Trying to keep it all in, stop it from slithering away, evading her. Steve gripped a hand around her throat and squeezed. He raised himself up on one arm, banging at her. It was like looking in a mirror. Their eyes desperate, locked. Their mouths tense, teeth feral, gritted and shining in the gleam of the street lamp.

Steve groaned, mumbled something she didn't quite catch.

Can't? Cunt. Yeah, talk dirty to me. She shivered, saw his mouth go slack, his eyes roll up in his head.

'Yes. Now!'

He collapsed, shuddering with gratitude, humping his orgasm into her. An imagined his white bottom making little pumping motions, bobbing away in the dark, and she laughed. In her fantasies she grunted and yelled her way through sex. In reality, location – always Steve's choice – and decorum decreed she be quiet. And anyway, what she felt when they had sex didn't match the pictures in her head, the sensations she had when she loved herself. So she panted, reserving her voice for the moment of penetration, and a laugh at the end. Steve seemed to like it. It let him know he'd given her a good time.

They lay, breathing, then, with tacit agreement, scrambled under the duvet and lay on their backs again, the bedding pulled up to their chins. Steve sat up. He fumbled for the bedside light and switched it on, revealing a dull little room with pale orange and cream striped wallpaper. He wrinkled his nose, eyes flickering around the walls. An took in the cracked sink, built into a makeshift bathroom unit; the brown cord carpet, worn and covered with fluff balls. No dead mice in evidence. Her gaze lingered on the black hand prints climbing up the wall beside the door.

'Where are my fags?' Steve had flung back the duvet, leaving her cold and exposed. She turned on her side.

'Your jeans are over here, look, they're in the pocket.'

He grunted his thanks. Lighting a slightly crumpled cigarette, he took a long drag then sighed the smoke out from between clenched teeth. He stood gazing out of the open window, into the early evening. He looked different naked.

Plumper, softer, paler. The muscles in his upper body were hard and well defined but immediately under his breastplate his body relaxed, became pouchy, prone to fat. His shoulders were pink as if he'd been sunning himself. His rounded tummy was white as lardy cake, rising and falling softly, making a little shelter for his pubic hair and his penis shrivelling in the cool air.

Steve looked at her, looking at him and winked. He came and sat beside her on the bed, one arm over her back. He crossed his legs and cocked his head at her, quizzical budgerigar.

'Post coital cigarette. Can't beat it.'

'Let's have a puff, then.'

'You don't smoke.' Steve seemed genuinely shocked. He held the cigarette away from her as if she might wrest it from him and choke herself on it.

'Ooops, so I don't. Quite right.' An snuggled nearer and looked at him under her lashes. She pouted. 'So what am I supposed to do, then?'

'Well, you could stay here. Enjoy the fabulous luxury of this unique hotel with its Central London location.' Steve got up and wedged the cigarette between his lips. He walked over to the sink. Grunting, he hitched himself up and began to piss. Looking up he caught her eye in the mirror, grinned and winked again.

'I've got to go, remember. Meeting someone. But the room's booked for the night. You may as well use it.'

She shivered and opened the porch door. She could use a long cool bath. Sleep. She felt grimy, disconnected. Music wafted out of the front room again. An stood in the unlit hall and waited for Beth's shout. Perhaps her sister hadn't heard her come in. She could just go straight upstairs and run the bath; come down later to say goodnight. But she was unlikely to get away with it; the noise of the iron grille was a harbinger proclaiming all arrivals. An put her shoulders back and her best foot forward, and entered the through-lounge.

As girls growing up they had hardly ever used the front room. Except for special occasions – visitors and Christmas – the family lived in the extension. Before that was built, when the through-lounge was still two rooms, they had used the dining room. Saturdays, while Mummy slept after doing her night shift at the hospital, the girls would spread paper and felt pens on the dining table. Spend the day drawing pictures or dancing to the top one hundred on Radio 1.

Mummy would get up to serve lunch, usually yesterday's left-overs or a tasteless, undressed salad, then go back to bed. And the house would return to its forced hush, the suppressed giggles and the shuffle of feet. They kept out of Daddy's way as much as possible.

The front room was Daddy's domain. He too spread paper: *The Times Educational Supplement*, magazine articles, stacks of 5M's homework. Mr Moore's English class. He sat cross-legged on the floor like a tailor, making and shaping 5M's compositions into a semblance of sense and grammatical correctness; tutting and shaking his head, creasing his brows in a frown that went all the way into his bald patch in a series of deep parallel lines.

Afterwards he would retire to his chair beside the china Pekingese. The stereo was an arm's stretch away, the standard lamp just behind his head. At his feet would be scattered cardboard filing boxes spilling over with cassettes. He would close his eyes and nod, straight-backed even in the easy chair.

This was what it was all about, the graft and the sacrifice. This made it all worthwhile. To sit in his chair, in his room, in his house, listening to 'the Classics'. Summoning his girls to come creeping, bearing cups of coffee, shop-bought cake. Willing legs to run errands; down the Broadway with his dry-cleaning or upstairs to the tallboy to fetch his cigars. Here, Mr Moore was as a king. He reigned supreme.

Beth was curled like a cat in Daddy's chair. The lamplight cast a soft gleam on her face; her eyes were closed. One hand, perched on the armrest, fluttered in time to the music.

An tiptoed into the room and folded herself into a corner of the settee. 'What's this, then?'

'Debussy.' Beth didn't open her eyes. She must have known An was in the room, must have been waiting for her to speak.

Their voices were low in the hallowed space. Suddenly it was Daddy's room again, imposing its authority over the new carpet, the rearranged furniture.

It was his music, that's what did it. The music demanded deference, just as he had. Not the melody itself – a skittish little tune that bounced along gaily, diving unexpectedly into hidden depths, sharps, minor chords – but the fact that it was classical music, with the weight of European refinement behind it. Pomp and circumstance. A man who listened to such music, who collected it, scouring the lending library and the radio listings for it, devoting hours to it – surely such a man had renounced his past? Conquered his humble origins, arrived in the lap of civilization?

An barked with laughter. A memory had flashed into her head. She and Dap, hand in hand, skipping over the polished parquet of the school hall wearing seersucker dresses with puff sleeves. Mincing and wiggling, clapping and curtseying while the teacher nodded her head in approval and tapped her foot to the beat.

'Music and mime. Miss Bennet, getting me and Dap to do a special performance. Da da da da da, da da da da.'

But what was the title? Something outrageous. She hadn't realised at the time but when she was a little older, nine or ten, she had cringed with shame at her unwitting collusion. She pointed at Beth. 'Got it! Gollywog's Cakewalk.'

Beth leaned forward and picked up the plastic cassette case. Daddy's writing scratched across the narrow lines, the pressure of pen dimpling the card. Beth squinted. 'So it is. Ten points.'

Beth leaned forward again until her hands touched the floor, her lower body still balancing in the armchair. She had painted her nails red today. Must have been going through An's things again. An watched as her sister's long fingers grazed through a filing box and pulled out another home recording. She slipped the tape into the old-fashioned stereo, fast-forwarded a little, pressed 'play', then sat back.

'Thirty seconds; what's this?'

A low, sweet note lilted into the room, swaying and bending, repeating itself. It grew louder, opened into a mournful melody. Together, Beth and An drifted their hands through the air in front of their faces.

'Ah, Rachmaninov. Piano Concerto Number 3, in D minor. Not to be confused with Number 2, more commonly known as the theme tune to that classic British weepie, *Brief Encounter*.'

'Very good!' Beth was surprised. 'You've been playing this game with your college friends.'

'Hardly. This was one of the first records I bought when I left home. I've got a whole pile of classical music, muddled in with Julian Joseph and Joan Armatrading. It's good stuff, but I thought you hated it.'

Beth shook her head. 'It makes me sad.' She uncurled a leg and kicked at the cardboard filing box. It toppled, sending cassettes scattering over the beige carpet. 'This makes me sad. The great collection.'

An dropped to her hands and knees and crawled over the floor until she sat beside her sister's chair. Handel's *Messiah*, 1981, 1982, 1983, two different recordings for 1984. These were the Christmas tapes, played every year before dinner, a tradition. And like all the best traditions, utterly pointless. Perhaps even he had realised this; after 1985 there was a gap of three years then one card indicated that four recordings had been made on the same tape, each one obliterated by the next. In another box the crabby black script noted songs by Paul Robeson and Cleo Laine. Several of these had been scratched out to be replaced by Britten and Prokofiev. Some of the tapes were simply labelled with the conductor's name, the date and time of performance. These Daddy had obviously taken from the radio, undoubtedly the Third Programme for which he reserved special reverence. Where were the Albinoni, Paganini, Ravel, Vivaldi, all the popular classics that she had heard as a child?

Beth broke into An's thoughts: 'Look, some of the blank ones are actually recordings but they start and finish in odd places. Like maybe he turned on the radio and heard something he liked and just taped it. No time to find out the composer or anything. Listen.'

She pressed 'play' and the insistent throb of Ravel's *Bolero* crackled out through the speakers.

*   *   *

Upstairs, An got into bed, pulled her rucksack onto her lap and rummaged round till she found the small brown paper parcel that Steve had given her. Too small to be a book; it had to be a cassette. Sure enough; a Stein's-own compilation tape, a sampler from the collection of the ultimate soul boy. An laughed, delighted. He had made his own cover to fit inside the box. Silver and gold writing on black card, each title embellished with a tiny star, a flower or a love heart. Music to make love to. A specialist's selection; she'd never heard of half these artists before she met Steve. It was the sweetest gesture; all the old favourites were there from when they were first going out. Songs he'd played for her the first time she went back to his bedsit, on their first date. And now, here they were again.

He had a way about him, Steve. Of pulling away from her then drawing her back again. In fact, their whole relationship had been like picking her way through a minefield. At any moment a life threatening obstacle could block her path. What if her parents found out? What if a passing stranger caught them having sex? What if Steve dumped her? The risk of that last occurrence was always there; his 'mood swings' were legendary. Adoring her one moment, ignoring her the next. From the beginning it was as though Steve kept her in a small compartment of his life. Never meeting his friends or family. Never seeing her more than once a week. He had run the show and An had accepted his rules. The mere thought of losing him used to make her heart stop.

An slipped the tape into her Walkman and put the headphones on. She snuggled down, examining the song titles as the first track purred into her ears.

When you're around you make me feel so good/ All of my worries so far away/ Then other times you make me feel so cold/ What makes you treat me this way?/ Can you feel the need in me?

Anita Baker, singing her story. Or rather, her history. She could see now that her own behaviour had been a large part of the problem. Always resisting him, trying to get more from him than he felt able to give. She was glad she understood him now. Of course he'd been afraid to commit himself before. What man wouldn't be? Everything had been so complicated and dramatic. There was the continuous subterfuge, just to spend an evening together. And then there was the passion, the intensity of their feelings for one another, just like this afternoon in the park. No wonder he had seemed so ambivalent.

. . . I need a little kindness/ A little tenderness/ A little love, somehow.

She was older and wiser. In a way, she should thank the breakdown. If she hadn't gone off the rails, hadn't been hospitalized, medicated, therapied, she wouldn't be the person she was now. Lying in this bed, in this house, seeing, understanding, accepting. Luther's warm voice wrapped itself around her. Closing her eyes, she sang along with him.

For every disappointment there is a compensation. This tape, for instance, was Steve's way of saying 'sorry'. It was obvious he would have liked to spend more time with her, wanted to be with her as much as she wanted to be with him. They would always have to snatch their moments, though. When she went back to college in October they'd be down to weekends and juggling residential shifts. Never mind. An pressed the stop button and turned the tape. She fast-forwarded through Opaz's 'Don't Say Nothing', onto her favourite track.

Did I tell you that I'm crazy?/ Crazy 'bout your love/ I know you understand exactly what I'm thinking of.

Yeah. Her man, Miles Jaye. Ambassador of love, for Stevie Stein.

This is my message to you/ I need you/ I need your love/ Oh baby, yes I do/ I never never ever ever want to be without you, oh girl . . .

An felt the happiness well up in her eyes and spill down her cheeks. She crossed her arms over her chest, rocking all the joy back into herself. She was suddenly reminded of that silly thing they used to do at school: where you stand facing a wall, wiggling and hugging yourself, so it looks to the people behind you as if someone else is running their hands up and down your back.

This is my message to you. I never ever want to be without you.

17
The Blood of an Englishman

On the counterpane in a shaft of light. Count the squares, one two three. He counts vertebrae, one two three. Each pane a way out. A window. There's a song sneaking about – like a window, you ain't got nothing but pain. How would they spell it, a-i-n or a-n-e? It's still raining, tears on the glass. There'll be a rainbow later, and at the end of it a pot of gold. He follows the curve of your back. Counting four five six . . . sixteen. Sweet sixteen. Are there really that many or is he pretending? It doesn't matter. Nothing matters.

It's warm in the light, almost cosy except his touch is bringing up goose bumps. You can't remember feeling goose bumps before. Or his touch. Why is this time different?

'This is the last time,' he says. 'I'm going to let you go. Fly away, little bird.' He laughs and starts at the top again, one two three all the way down to sixteen. Another song.

'Happy Birthday, Sweet Sixteen.'

His voice surprises you, mellow and rich. He sounds like Paul Robeson. He even looks a bit like him, in the pictures of him as a young man. You can't remember him singing to you before. But this time is different, like no other. This is the last time.

'Go on, then.'

He says it gruffly but his hand, as he pushes you off the bed, is gentle. He turns away from you, hugged around himself. The word mollusc comes to mind. No backbone. He does many things to you, he is many things but he never lies. This is the last time.

He says, 'You're lovely, Neets,' sweet and low, his voice smoky with the breath of his cigarette. Blows thin streams of cloud up to the ceiling and leaves his lips pursed, savouring the words. His face beside yours on the pillow, he winks at you and smiles.

What, in particular, have you done that was lovely? Is it the way one eye goes sleepy after sex, or the high points of your nipples peering over the sheet? Maybe the way your teeth protrude when you lie down, and you have to lick under your lips to pull your mouth down over them. Practise this move, watch for his reaction. He gazes at you, expression unrevealed, and goes on smoking.

He says all the things he has ever wanted to say and he says them to you. He says, 'my dusky angel'. He says, 'you're so fucking sexy', 'get naked', 'God, you're beautiful, I'm going to screw your arse off. I'm going to screw you blind'. He says these things to you, and more. He talks dirty to you, mouthing hot words in your ear while he works your hand over his body, down and round and up, down and round and up.

You say, 'I love you, Stevie.' I love you. Love me. Love me too.

18

Fantasy Island

Beth lies on the bed, eyes closed. Her lashes rest on her cheeks, glossy and curled at the ends like on a sleeping cherub. She doesn't flinch as the pillow settles over her, sinking into the contours of her face, pushing down, pushing out the air.

An shifts herself to get better leverage. Full weight on her arms now, she grips the pillow in both hands and leans into it.

A long, ticking pause, the clock keeping watch with An in the silence.

Then Beth begins to kick. She bangs her palms on the mattress, tries to turn her head but it's wedged tightly under the pillow. Her heels shoot up, down, one after the other, like she's riding a bike fast. Then, from somewhere, she finds a thin high note, unearthly as a cat crying in the dark, and projects it over the deadening embrace of the pillow. An lifts her hands, gesturing innocence. Beth bolts upright, raised from the dead. She covers her face with her hands and breathes and breathes. Her mouth hangs ragged, hungry.

'Bloody hell, An, that was a long time. How long?'

'I forgot to count but it wasn't long.'

'Not for you, maybe.' Beth flings the pillow to the floor, scrambles to her knees, eager and eyes shining. 'Come on then, it's my turn.'

An whines, 'Oh, you're going to get your own back.'

'I won't.'

'You will.'

'Well, it's my turn, anyhow. You'll just have to trust me.'

Reluctantly, An stands up, exchanging places. She lies down on the bed with her arms at her sides.

'Lift up.'

She lifts her head and Beth passes the stockings under her neck.

'Not too tight.' An fingers the brown nylon nervously. The stockings smell of hair oil and cocoa butter.

'Now close your eyes,' Beth orders. With a practised flick of the wrist, she wraps a length of nylon around each fist. Crosses her arms and savagely pulls.

The room was light by four o'clock, bright by six. Unable to sleep any longer, Beth sat up and swung her feet onto the floor. Already, through the open window, she could hear the rush of the motorway. She could just lie there and rest of course, let the sound lull her – she hadn't had more than a few hours' sleep – but she knew what she'd be like if she didn't get up. After a while she'd start dozing and having all kinds of peculiar dreams. Then her body would get heavy, she wouldn't be able to lift her head from the pillow. Before she knew it, it would be midday and she'd be ravenous and the day would go by in a lethargic stupor of eating and slouching around in her nightclothes. She shuddered. Best to get up with the start of the day; besides, there were chores waiting.

In the bathroom, she splashed her face with cold water and brushed her teeth. She found an old pair of leggings in the bottom of the washbasket and retrieved yesterday's T-shirt. She sniffed her armpits before putting it on. A bit frowsy; she could have a shower later, when she'd finished her work and was sweaty. When she'd earned it. First, a cup of tea, to wake herself up. At the top of the stairs, Beth paused, head cocked towards her sister's room. Then she trotted lightly down in her towelling slippers.

The house was still and cool. In the hallway red and green shapes arched across the walls, rivalling the geometric pattern of the wallpaper and the reflected curlicues of the door grille – morning was streaming through the stained-glass window beside the door. The mirrors hung opposite each other, ticking lightly from side to side as if someone had just rushed past and moved them. Beth reached out her arms; she tapped a fingernail into the centre of each mirror, and waited until they were still. It was the vibration from the motorway. Barely audible in itself, it set mirrors swaying, wine glasses tinkling, water splashing in the sink.

Beth bestrode the hall like a colossus. She tipped back her head and drew a deep breath. This was the best time of day, Mummy was right. Before the house woke up, before the demands began. When it was just her and the chores and she could work her way steadily through each task, in control of her world. Maybe she wouldn't worry about working again. Maybe she'd stay here and keep house with Mummy. Just the two of them, after Anita went back to college. It would be peaceful. Orderly. She'd be like a . . . what was the word? She'd become a contemplative.

Smiling to herself, Beth moved around the downstairs rooms opening doors, Venetian blinds and windows. To think she used to be so ambitious; getting her degree and a good job were once the only things that made sense – that and George. When George got sent down the ambition went too. All her courage, her drive, her optimism: sent down. It would have been different if she were not pregnant. She would have managed, bounced back, rallied her resources. Five years was a long time, but hardly an eternity. She would have visited. Made sure he kept up with his education. Found a university near the prison and, when the time came, found a flat for them both. George would have had something to keep him going while he was away. The thought of her, waiting for him, working – for them. With good behaviour he would have been out in two years. And at least he was away from his Mum. No prison regime could possibly be harsher than Mrs Goode.

The baby, however, was a fact. It couldn't be wished – or cursed – away. Even before he was sentenced Beth had known what she must do. She had pictured herself, floating down the proverbial creek without a paddle, trailing her hands in the effluent, drifting on alone. Stinking and abandoned. And, with horror, had returned to the only safety she knew.

She couldn't say she'd been wrong. Her life had turned out alright. She'd got the degree. The career was there to be had if she wanted it. More importantly, she had the support of her best friend – her mother. And given what had become of George, she was surely vindicated.

Returning to the kitchen, she put the kettle on to boil and got the bucket and mop out. She'd start here first, at the centre of the house, and radiate out: through-lounge, extension and hall, in that order. As she sipped her tea, Beth let her mind wander again. Yes, things could always be worse. She had dreaded An's return, for instance. Perhaps An having missed Mummy had been a good thing. She and An would only have quarrelled – they always did. Mummy would have gone on holiday upset and Beth would have been left to smooth things over with her sister.

There had been a time when An was Mummy's favourite, a long time ago, when they were small. Mummy had never said as much. In fact, she'd always prided herself on treating her daughters in exactly the same way.

'What's good enough for one of unu is good enough for all.'

So they wore matching dresses and hair ribbons, got the same sweets at the same time. If one was smacked, it was smacks all round. Totally unfair. But Beth saw the way Mummy had treated An when she thought Beth wasn't looking. Stroking her hair, petting her, sneaking her toffees with a wink and a grin, whispering endearments.

Later on, Beth was avenged. The parents swapped allegiances and An became Daddy's girl, while Beth had Mummy all to herself. Sometimes, on the evenings she didn't work, Mummy would stretch out on the sofa and pat the narrow space beside her, beckoning Beth to her with a sleepy smile. They would lie there, ostensibly watching the television. But out of the corner of her eye, Beth would watch An. Hunched down in her chair, a sour expression turned towards the flickering screen, An would sit until she couldn't stand the exclusion any more. Then she would leap up, declaring, 'I'll just see if Daddy wants anything.'

They'd let her go, every time. Glad to be rid of her.

'Your sister's too much trouble,' Mummy used to whisper. 'Leave her to her Daddy. He knows how to handle her.' And certainly An seemed quieter under Daddy's tutelage. Not so full of herself. Not so much lip. Those years had been almost happy for Beth. She wasn't bothered that An seemed to grow quieter and more nervous every year; that Mummy clearly held her youngest child in contempt. If it hadn't been for Greta, Beth's pre-pubescent and early teenage years would have passed in a wave of contentment.

Smug bitch. That's what Greta used to call her. Greta would hide her doll, call her a big baby, slap her when she cried. Greta would send her to Coventry, telling An in a loud voice to 'lock the bedroom door. We don't want traitors here. Run to Mummy, traitor, we don't care.' Years later, it had been Greta's idea to write to the Lonely Hearts. Since An went to a girls' school it was the only way to get a boyfriend, she insisted. So, in a way, Greta had brought Steve and An together. Her hand was visible in every aspect of An's life.

Beth kissed her teeth. Of course it was. If she wasn't careful she'd end up in the madhouse herself. Greta was An, An was Greta. She'd made her up, just like they'd made up the Franklins; and Raven, Skinflint and Fox. Making them so real – every nuance, every characteristic – she could picture them in her mind's eye.

Greta had been the most convincing. She could see her, swaggering into the kitchen, tossing her head in such a way that Beth almost believed there was a mane of black hair falling over her shoulders. She was the one who'd told Mummy about the abortion. She was the one who'd earned Beth the most awful beating of her life. That's how Beth had known An's secret; that Greta was back after An had promised them she was gone. Shot herself in the foot that time. The truce was over. Beth had searched and searched until she found An's diary.

It was strange, after the abortion. Mummy didn't carry out her threat to tell Daddy. Beth would be lying beside his pot of ashes in the garden of remembrance now if she had. He would have had to act if he had been told. But he must have known; when her milk came in, he *must* have known. Daddy, it seemed, didn't care. Beth was not his business. He'd lowered his newspaper to watch the milk spray from her breasts, over the breakfast. His expression remained unchanged. Then he'd raised *The Times* up to his face again, flicked his wrists so the paper gave an eloquent crack! and never said another word about it.

An had been beside herself with fright, Beth remembered. It was two days before she stopped shaking. Greta had nearly gone too far then. But it wasn't long before she'd turned An's head again. Everything was soon back to normal.

Normal! Beth jumped to her feet as if Greta had appeared before her. She shook her head furiously, trying to dispel the image of An's 'twin'. Picking up the mop-bucket, she filled it under the hot water tap and swished cleaning fluid into it until suds sloshed onto the floor. Normal! When had things ever been normal? Beth pushed the mop across the lino, flung it away from herself and pulled it back, tussling with it.

Revenge. Retribution. That's what it had been. A constant battle to keep ahead of the game, to dish the greatest amount of dirt, and cause the other maximum trouble. The house had become a war-zone. No trick was too low. Diaries were read, false amnesties declared, violence was committed. And all the spoils were offered to Mummy and Daddy; her sister's head on a plate. First she got rid of Greta. Then she'd begun the slow process of getting rid of An. It had taken a long time. Beth had left home and gone to university by then. But she had unfinished business with An.

Beth had been thorough. She always was. She prided herself on a job well done. It had been Mummy's mantra. 'A job worth doing . . .' Beth washed herself into a corner, pulling the mop in her wake. Then she set it upright in the bucket, stepped back into the extension and admired her gleaming floor.

'What's going on?'

'Greta, thank God you're here. Mummy's laying into Beth. Listen.'

Crouched together at the top of the stairs, your hands clutching the banisters, straining your ears towards the sounds. Angry footsteps in the kitchen pace up and down, up and down. Abruptly they stop.

'You're disgusting, dirty,' Mummy's voice hisses into the silence. 'In all my born days I never, never expected this . . .' trails off into a furious mutter and the pacing begins again. Next a cascade of water; you hear it gurgle and splutter down the drain, then the whine of the hot tap and the slap of water collecting in a metal bucket.

'Plenty of soap. Enough! Now the bleach, I want this kitchen spotless. Then you'll learn about decency. I'll teach you to bring dirt into this house.'

This is scary. They've been in there for over an hour with the door shut. Beth must have cleaned the room from ceiling to floor and up again. But Beth did the kitchen two days ago. What dirt, there isn't any dirt. Unless . . .

'Abortion! Abortion!'

It's a growl, a howl of agony. It brings sharp rapid slaps, a smothered cry of pain. And finally her voice rises unlike anything you've ever heard before.

'You filthy little BITCH, you nasty dirty BITCH.' Beating in time to her words, rising and falling like a prayer.

You and Greta are one person; you stumble down the stairs, crash into the kitchen. Beth, face down in a soapy puddle, drinking in bleach water with every shuddering breath. Above her towers Mummy, ugly with vengeance, fists clenched on her hips.

'I can smell you from here,' she moans, and shoves her foot in Beth's face.

'What are you doing?'

An stood in the middle of the lino and rubbed the sleep out of her eyes. Beth, wobbling at the top of the little stepladder, almost fell.

'Christ, An. You can see what I'm doing, don't be stupid.'

An watched her sister reach up to the window again and fumble at the top of the curtains. She was trying to unhook the nets, only the wire was strung as taut as it could be and the tiny eyelet would not slide off the equally tiny hook embedded in the window frame. Grunting, Beth stretched the wire out with both hands. It extended that vital two milli-metres, popped off the hook and Beth leapt to the floor as the ladder toppled over.

'Looks dangerous to me.'

Beth ignored her. Shrugging, An lifted the kettle to check

there was enough water for tea then switched it on. Beth pulled the plastic-covered wire through the hem at the top of the net curtain. She dropped the curtain on the carpet and carefully put the coil of wire on the table. It stretched out, a lazy snake, dangling off the table in a limp line.

'Why're you washing the curtains?'

Beth kissed her teeth sharply. 'Because they're dirty, of course.'

'Look spotless to me.' An shuffled her bare feet into the extension. She picked up the discarded curtain and examined it. The hem was grubby where the voile had trailed among the pot plants littering the window sill. Otherwise, they were glitteringly white. Beth picked up the steps and huffed her way across the room to the second window. An eyed her speculatively as Beth stretched up and prepared to repeat the painful procedure with the curtain wire.

'You could always just wash the bottom, you know. Like, put a bowl of soapy water on the window sill. Save yourself a lot of trouble. I mean, that really doesn't look safe, what you're doing . . .'

'An!' Beth's bellow echoed round the room. She jumped off the ladder again, leaving the wire jumping and the net bouncing.

'I was only trying to . . .'

'What the hell do you know about it? Huh?' Beth stood where she had landed, hands clenched by her sides. She looked as if she would like to advance upon An and cause her a serious mischief. 'You can't just wash a *bit* of something. Didn't you do any housework before, or what? You'd get water marks, thickhead.'

She kissed her teeth again, a long, syrupy contemptuous

note. She managed to unhook the second curtain and, retrieving the first, put them both in the washing machine. Back in the extension, she set up the ironing board. As soon as the iron was warm she began banging away at a clean pair of nets.

'D'you want tea?' An's voice was careful, solicitous. It riled her. Why were people always talking to her like she was a child? Like they had to watch what they said or she might break? She wasn't the one who'd flipped. The doctor had never given her drugs to calm her down. She wasn't the one who was an attention-seeking little cow. She was fine.

She was losing it; her hand, on the iron, trembled.

Mug in hand, An settled herself in one of the easy chairs near her sister. Beth glanced at her. 'Put the telly on, *The Flying Doctors* has just started.'

'Oh you *don't* watch that do you?' An laughed. 'Day-time telly is so sad. Beth, you should get out more. Get a life.'

Beth banged the iron down, walked around the board and switched on the television. The news was on; *The Flying Doctors* was on another channel. She looked about for the remote control, finally spying it tucked inside An's chair, where she herself had been sitting a couple of days ago.

'Pass it.'

An handed it over with a quiet smile. 'You could come out with me if you wanted to. My friend Eloise is giving a big party in Brixton next weekend. You can wear your new dress. The one with the flowers on? It's really nice. You never know; might meet a nice bloke there?'

The ironing board crashed to the floor. Before she realised what she was doing, Beth was leaning over her sister, the iron centimetres from An's cheek.

'Back off.' Little flecks of spittle hit the hot metal and sizzled out. 'Back off and get out of my face or, I swear, I'll burn yours right off.'

An fled.

19

Scylla and Charybdis

It was a wooden tray with six coasters, each with a different design on it. According to her mood, Mummy had either picked it up in a junk shop or been given it as a leaving present Back Home. In any case, the tray set dated back to the fifties or early sixties. It was made of a light, cheap wood, heavily varnished, but the varnish had been breached by successive scourings; now the sticky crusts of indeterminate substances clung to its corners, and milky stains permeated the wood.

Sunlight, misuse and age had faded the motifs painted onto the coasters: cocktail glasses, skinny women in full skirts and s-bend hairstyles, bunches of fruit. One coaster bore the legend, 'Here's mud in your eye!' with a drawing of a funny face. The meaning was obscure but presumably it was some kind of drinking salute, like, 'Cheers!' 'Bottoms Up!' 'Down the Hatch!' Most of the others had been rubbed into oblivion but she remembered them all.

Her favourite was on the tray itself. Daddy, with his fondness for maxims, mottoes and homilies, had liked it too. On at least two occasions he had taken a pot of red paint and one of black from the vast dusty store at the back of the shed.

Then he'd trim to fine points two sable artists' brushes and lay them carefully on the kitchen table. He would spread newspaper on the table and place the tray on top. Next came a rag soaked in turpentine, and a dry cloth. Then, tongue poking from the corner of his mouth, he would laboriously stroke the brushes over the lettering on the tray. First a red letter then a black, until the words stood out in glistening fresh paint: 'A Camel Can Live In The Desert For Thirty Days Without Water . . .'

In the bottom right hand corner, its neck stretching into the centre of the tray, stood the camel. Once Daddy had given him a 'touch up' as well and he now had a roguish air to him, the floppy hair of his mane askew, a wicked, Daddy-ish glint in his eye. They used to laugh about this as girls. A camel with Daddy's face. Ruminative, rather stupid. It rendered Daddy harmless to see him there, with his four legs and his hairy hump, smiling up through the base of a glass.

At the very bottom of the tray, sloping down from left to right, was the rest of the phrase . . . 'But Who Wants To Be A Camel?!' The paint had dribbled under the question mark and, despite Daddy's rubbing at it with the turps, it had stained. A smudge of red bled into the wood.

Beth scratched at the stain with her index finger. Her red nail varnish – An's nail varnish – was beginning to chip, the dark ivory of her fingernail peeping through the scarlet. There was something, something she couldn't quite get hold of, just floating about in the air above her head. A revelation. Beth frowned and looked up as if expecting to see a thought bubble bobbing in front of her. No, the more she tried to recall it the more it eluded her. Whatever 'it' was.

She would forgo the doily and the cocktail sticks. Just two

tall glasses, brimming with lemonade. And some buttered brioche. An would be hungry. Beth arranged the crockery carefully so that the glasses and plate made a frame for the camel's face. Then slowly she climbed the stairs to the back bedroom.

It was a surprise to find the room empty. She had expected to see An huddled on the bed, sobbing. Or else packing her suitcase. Instead the room was silent and shadowy. The blinds were up, the window open and a stiff breeze brought goosebumps up on Beth's arms. She put the tray on top of the dressing table and looked around. Really, there was only one place else An could be.

Beth knocked on the shiny green door. When there was no reply she pushed it open and went to sit on the bed beside her sister. An did not acknowledge her. She continued gazing around their parents' room, a look of bewildered astonishment on her face.

'This is where he died,' Beth said, turning to indicate Daddy's side of the bed. The counterpane, the same counterpane that had been on the bed that day, lay soft and fluffy, cascading to the floor in a sweep of pale peach honeycombs.

Mummy had had instructions, after Daddy died. Her father had called her from Jamaica, the first time Beth could ever remember this happening. He had not wasted precious seconds with small talk; he had been very specific. Mary was to find a tape measure, a cloth one, and tie it around her waist. She must wear this under her clothes for at least ten days, together with a pair of red knickers. Red silk knickers, no others would do. Then she was to strip the bed in which her husband had died and burn all the bedding. Never mind the waste. It was important. She must do exactly as he said. She must open the windows wide and tie up the curtains.

Lastly she must rearrange the bedroom furniture so that if the ghost lost its way to the other side and tried to return, it would not recognize the room.

Mummy had followed her daddy's orders to the letter. When Beth asked her what she was doing she had laughed, clearly embarrassed. 'It's a Back Home thing; you modern generation wouldn't understand. Come, help me move this bed under the window.'

But she had drawn the line at destroying the counterpane. It was a good one, she argued (more to herself than to her bemused daughter). She'd bought it on a trip to Paris during her student days; it had cost a small fortune but in those days she had only herself to spend her money on. Even then she could spot quality when she saw it. It wasn't often she indulged herself, not like your Dad, but she had that one time and the spread meant a lot to her. It was older than Beth. You couldn't get them like that anymore.

Beth wondered if the existence of the counterpane meant there was a channel left open for Daddy's ghost to return. 'He wouldn't dare!'

Startled, An looked at her.

'Daddy,' Beth explained. 'He wouldn't dare haunt us. He knows better than to show his face around here.'

An smiled tentatively, then she grinned. Beth was staring at the pillow, a deep frown scouring her features as if she could see the old man himself lying in the bed.

'Get thee behind me, Satan,' An said in a melodramatic whisper. She sputtered and covered her mouth with a hand. Giggling, they hunched together at the foot of the bed, ssshh-ing and batting at each other until the fit was over.

'Aieeee!' An kicked up her heels and flung herself backwards. She swung her legs up and down like a child and looked around the room. Like the other bedrooms, it was almost exactly the same as when she had last seen it. Her parents' room had only undergone one transformation in her lifetime (apart from the temporary one immediately preceding Daddy's funeral). Now she saw the same embossed wallpaper Daddy had put up when she and Beth were children. The carpet, a rich floral Axminster, was getting threadbare. The white melamine fitted robes, that Daddy had made himself, had yellowed with age. Only the curtains were new and they were clearly homemade. Mummy specials, with an uneven ruffled pelmet that dangled off one end of the curtain rail.

Beth saw her staring and said defensively, 'They're just a try-out. Mummy had the fabric lying around. We'll get round to doing upstairs after Christmas. We didn't want too much disruption whilst . . .'

'It's brought you even closer, hasn't it?'

It was the mildest of questions, asked in the mildest of tones. Still, Beth felt herself getting hot in the face. 'An . . .'

'It's alright, you know. I understand.' An smiled. 'All those hours of therapy haven't gone entirely to waste.'

That was it: the revelation. Something she had known all along and only now understood. An was the one who had got away. The one who had had a chance to grow up, to decide her own truths rather than having to live with the ones Mummy and Daddy had handed down. For An, coming home was not necessarily a time to face up to the past. Perhaps she had already done so and it was Beth who was lagging behind.

But look at An now, lying on the bed smiling, as if life was a sweet rose and all she had to do was sniff it. As if she hadn't just come within a whisker of being scarred for life. After everything she'd been through, An was smiling.

Beth lay down beside her sister and propped herself up on her elbows. Something was required of her, she knew. She was hesitating outside the confessional, the curtain raised, rehearsing her lines. How could she say it? If only you hadn't been so troublesome; if you had just cried a bit more and fought a bit less. If you hadn't been so stuck up, so unreachable. If only there had not been Greta. Maybe then Beth could have helped her. Been able to take her part, protect her, even. That was her job, surely, as the Big Sister? But An had turned against her too. Scorned her, humiliated her, injured her. How could she say it? If it wasn't for you we would be a normal family. All my life I've blamed you. I still blame you. The desire to strike An, to obliterate her, and the urge to prostrate herself at her sister's feet begging forgiveness, battled within her. An admission was clearly impossible; an invitation, then.

'He. Daddy. He used to do things to you, didn't he?'

'You read my diary, Beth. What do you want me to say?'

Something else she had known all along. She even had an idea of when it had started, although it wasn't until she'd found the diaries, written from the time An was about twelve, that that particular memory had made sense. She used to revel in the knowledge; it was a comfort whenever she felt jealous of An's status with Daddy. That at least she didn't have to do things. She didn't have to run, trembling, whenever Daddy called. And re-emerge, grey faced, and spend hours in the bathroom washing and re-washing her hands. So, if she knew, Mummy . . .

They'd been reading comics one day. *Beano* for Beth; An still liked *Twinkle*; sprawled across the twin beds, only the odd giggle breaking the silence. Lost in comic heaven, Beth didn't hear him coming. By the time he pushed open the door An was standing to attention beside her bed; Pierrot lay crying; *Twinkle* was nowhere to be seen. As quietly as she could Beth had stuffed the soft paper down the front of her jumper. Comics were forbidden. But he wasn't even looking at her.

'Lisa-Beth, your mother's calling you.' He held open the door, eyes fixed on An. Gratefully, Beth squeezed past him, holding her bulky front, rustling faintly. He shut the door behind her, still without a word to An. Just as it closed she saw her sister's face. Blank as a scrubbed blackboard.

Mummy was in the kitchen, listening to *Desert Island Discs*. Apples lay neatly in a dish, waiting to be turned into apple cake.

'Yes, Mum?'

Mummy beat the batter for the cake in time to the music.

'Daddy said you wanted me.'

Mummy turned, frowned with irritation. 'He must be hearing things, I never called you. Cho, child, go away and leave me in peace.'

Then they heard a bang, resonant, abrupt, like something heavy falling to the floor. Mummy switched off the radio. They stood, staring at the ceiling, waiting. Mummy's cake-making hand made three slow circuits of the bowl and stopped. The tableau held for just a moment, then . . .

'What are An and Daddy doing upstairs?'

Suddenly Mummy was a whirl of motion. Radio on, batter poured out and cake in the oven. She tossed Beth a potato. 'What are you standing there like a fool for? Can't you see there's a million and one things to do? Make a start on the vegetables or we'll be having lunch at midnight.'

Beth began to cry, long shuddering sobs that shook the bed. Water streamed from her eyes and nose. A long line of spittle fell onto the bed and bled a dark shadow onto the counterpane.

An sighed. There was nothing she could do. No comfort to be offered. She patted her sister's shoulder awkwardly and retreated to her own room. There she found the tray with the breakfast; she ate and drank, listening to Beth's howls of anguish in the next room. She bathed, dressed, put on her make-up. When she saw her next, Beth was coming out of the downstairs shower room, refreshed and fully composed.

They had brunch in the garden in near silence. Neither of them was hungry; they did little more than pick at the sausages, fried plantain and toast. But it was the first meal the sisters had prepared together in years. It was oddly consoling to see the food, glistening and hearty on the plates before them.

They were like people who have survived a major disaster; unsure that they have survived or that the disaster has even taken place. Several times that day An caught Beth standing in the middle of a room, her chin uplifted and her eyes blank, listening to some inner voice. Then she would shake her head, as if in wonder, and move slowly on. An felt light and loose; untethered. She had the unmistakable feeling that she had missed something; of having bailed out in the right place at the wrong time. For the rest of the day she tried to pin it down but instead her head floated free from her body. It was impossible to think about just now.

Finally, they were like new lovers. Charmed with one

another, almost happy, but diffident, vaguely anxious. At the end of the day An said to Beth, 'Goodnight, dear,' and touched her lightly on the arm.

It was her turn to get up in the night and stand outside the bedroom door. The sounds she heard were alarming. Moaning and banging, long muttered chants, praying. Beth was grieving. An leaned her forehead against the door and, for the second time since coming home, she too began to weep. Ah, Bethel, this was just the start. It truly was between a rock and a hard place her poor sister now found herself.

But Beth's dreams that night were not of mountainous landscapes or stark lunar terrains. Instead she dreamt of an island. A lush, tropical place where the foliage was poisonous and the air burned her lungs. She was stranded on a strip of molten sand without shelter or shade. Out across the bay a beautiful sea churned. She had never been there before, she was sure of it, but everything was as familiar as if she'd spent her life there. Beth knew with absolute certainty that at the mouth at the bay, where it gave onto the open sea, was a whirlpool. Fathoms deep, hundreds of fathoms. And beside it, leaving a passage barely wide enough for a single strong swimmer, lurched a hideous sea monster.

20

Bedside Manners

'Go and get her then, go on, na. Prove it.'

Mummy's singsong, like the girls in the playground, go on, dare you. Hands folded under her Cross-Your-Heart chest, she puffs herself up like a bullfrog. Dare.

'I don't have to. Greta can speak for herself.'

'Greta can't do *shit*.' From your mother's mouth, the curse is shocking. 'You said you finished with all that nonsense when you turned sixteen. You promised me. How can I ever trust you again? You've had more licence than is good for you, that's your trouble. Well this is where it ends.'

'Greta, Greta,' Beth takes up the chorus. Later, you'll wipe that smirk right off her face. She started this, couldn't leave it alone, could she? Always pushing it, always poking around.

'She's been snooping in my things. She read my diary. Bitch!'

'I never. Mummy, tell her! She can't talk to me like that.'

'Oh, is this you mean?' Mummy goes into the larder, comes out with a notebook. Grey, spiral-bound, yours.

'Give it me.'

Beth backs into the corner, laughing. She's practically

sticking out her tongue. Stupid baby, you and Greta'll get her for this.

'It's all lies,' she says. 'You're disgusting. You'd have to be sick to think up those things.' Screws up her face like she's sucking a gobstopper and has just now got to the bitter aniseed in the middle.

Mummy's holding your diary like a trophy. 'Never mind that. What I'm concerned about is this Steve character. Because it seems to me that you're planning on going the same way as your sister here.'

Ha! Beth hangs her head, shamed. Her fists give her away, and her mouth, tight with fury. Sorely mistaken if she thought she could get back in favour so soon. Mummy's wagging finger reminds her; that abortion was unforgivable. She'll have to do better than this before it can be forgotten.

Meanwhile, she has you to deal with. 'So you tell me about that boy, you tell me the truth NOW or I'll go straight into that front room and show this to your dad.'

She's bluffing; she wouldn't dare. If she's read it, she'd never want him to see it. Then the game would be up. Even if he calls you a liar, even if he says you made it up, all of it, for all those years, she'd look in his eyes and she'd know; and she really doesn't want to know. So it's your turn.

'Dare.'

She bugs her eyes at you, looks away, looking at Beth.

'She can't help you now, lady. Just you and me.'

'Well I . . . I . . . I . . .'

Gotcha! Mummy's blush spreads under her skin like blood in a puddle. She can't touch you, there's not a damn thing she can do. 'This is ridiculous.' You kiss your teeth, snatch back the book, and Beth starts to shout.

'How dare you talk to Mummy like that, you're a disgrace.'

And Mummy starts to scream, 'You and your nastiness. Your head so full of filth you can't study, you can't sleep. Stevie, Stevie, Stevie all night long. I've heard you, in your room, moaning and I don't know what. You're gonna fin' yourself up shit creek, fast; y'hear me, Anita, you better stop right now.'

And there's a wind at your back and a rushing noise and whump! the air's knocked out of you. You'd fall down but he's dragging you up again, out into the hallway, burning your legs on the carpet. Shaking you the way he shakes his macintosh out after the rain. He'll break your neck, he'll kill you this time.

'Bernard!'

Why is she screaming? This is it, isn't it – what she wanted? He's got his hands everywhere. He's scratching and pinching, pushing you down. One foot on your back; the lion, vanquished. And he's doing that thing with his trousers, hitching them up, scrabbling at the belt buckle, pulling the strap through the loops so fast it must burn.

'Greta.' Please come. They'd have to stop if she was here. 'Greta.' You'll laugh about this later, about Mummy and Beth clinging to each other like wet cats in a shipwreck, mewling. 'Greta.' Why won't she come. Sister? Help me please. 'Greta.' You say her name for every lash. You hope he scars you. You hope he goes on and on until you faint. You'll never betray her. 'Greta.' Never. With every stripe she'll know how much you love her.

She didn't come. There has to be a reason. She's as real as you are and she always comes when you call her. Some superhuman power helps you off the hall floor, drags you like a kitten by the scruff of your neck, up the stairs, screamingly slow. Nothing in your head but pain, and the need to get there. You burst through the door. She's face down on the bed, hair a wave of midnight hiding her from view, secreting her. She's already gone. A feeling, something unnameable, drenches you from head to foot as soon as you set eyes on her. It's not just the pills, spilling onto the carpet, red on red. It's the way she's curled away from you, in a way she never would in life. In death, she rejects you.

She's right; you are to blame. Already, you miss her.

The house looked liked Laurel and Hardy had been to visit for the weekend; the mess was unbelievable: puddles on the floor, drips from the ceiling, flour up the walls. So much broken. If she could have cared she would have laughed. She'd never liked Laurel and Hardy much; a mindless maelstrom. She always found herself worrying about the person whose home they were trashing. How they'd feel when they opened the front door. Wondering how they'd ever sort it out. Now she knew why they called it a fine mess. It was better than fine. Superb. Superlative. And she'd done it all by herself.

An huddled in her bed, fully dressed. Plum tomatoes, and sugar and something brown dribbled from her T-shirt onto the duvet. Obliterating Pierrot. Her breath came in erratic gasps. Her eyelids felt heavy. Soon she'd be asleep and when she woke up none of it would have happened. Her whole life would have been a dream. She knew the flickering shadow outside the open door was Mummy. Wringing her hands. Frightened. Really shitting herself this time. An lay back in the bed and, smiling, closed her eyes.

She was woken by a knocking on her bedroom door and Mummy calling, 'The doctor's here.' She added, 'Go on in, Doctor Shaw. I'll just be downstairs if you need me. I'll put the kettle on.'

Dr Shaw bowed into the room wearing a dickie bow and a disapproving smile.

He put his bag on the floor and rasped his hands together. 'Well, young lady, you've exceeded yourself this time. Sit up, please. What's brought it on, hmmmmm? Premenstrual? Boyfriend trouble? Row with your parents?' Talking all the while, he examined her. He pushed up her eyelids with a broad thumb, shone a light into each of her eyes. Then he peered into her throat, into her ears, felt the glands in her neck. Perhaps he would announce that she had nothing more than a nasty dose of flu. Affects people in different ways, you know. Some sneeze, some go berserk.

'Now, let's see what's really going on, shall we?' Dr Shaw chafed his palms again. He looked at her benignly, over the top of his little gold-rimmed glasses. He bent towards her and put one hand over each of her breasts. Dr Shaw made soothing, doctorly noises in the back of his throat; he clicked his tongue and tutted as he kneaded An's chest. A sheen of sweat covered his face. Placing one hand between her shoulder blades, he slipped the other under the bedclothes.

'There now,' he said. 'Good, very good.'

When he had finished he stood up straight and crossed his arms. He tapped a finger on his lips, thoughtfully. It was the same finger he had used to probe her. An stared at the finger, bouncing gently against his mouth. She lay down and turned her face away.

'I'm just going to give you a little injection. Help you to

sleep. And I'll leave a prescription with Mum. Now, we'll have no more nonsense. Hmmm?'

She heard them murmuring together in the kitchen. Then the doctor's cheery, 'goodbye,' as Mummy showed him out. It seemed an age before she heard her mother's slow footsteps on the stairs. Her eyelids were heavy again, her limbs like stone. At last Mummy stood beside the bed, looking down at her. Her yellow-brown face was clear and unafraid, her confidence restored. Through the fug of medication An thought she saw a gleam of triumph in her mother's eyes.

'He touched me.' Her tongue moved like a salted slug in her mouth, thick, ready to burst. She tried again, 'He touched me.'

Mummy's face froze. 'Who touched you? No-one touched you.'

'Here. He put his hands here, and under here.'

'Be quiet. It's the drugs talking.' Mummy stroked a hand over An's brow and straightened the dirty duvet. 'Nothing happened, it's all in your head.'

She busied herself between the bedroom and the bathroom, sponging An's face and neck, changing the bedlinen, helping An into a clean nightdress. She did it all with the loving efficiency that only a nurse could summon.

Just as she stood at the bedroom door for the last time, An roused herself. 'Dr Shaw touched me.' The words were very distinct. An let her head fall back on the pillow, let her eyes close. From very far away she heard Mummy.

'Oh, the *doctor*.' Her relief was tangible. She laughed, giddily. 'What makes you think a big man like Dr Shaw would fancy a silly little girl like you?'

21

Almost Blue

Embankment Station, a walk by the river and a meal at Gar-funkel's. All the ingredients, in the right order; they were back on track. Steve looked up as the waitress put the bowls on the table in front of him.

She smiled. 'Enjoy your meal, sir.'

'I'm sure your worthy establishment will afford us an excellent repast.'

Steve craned his head to watch her as she walked to the back of the restaurant, shaking her blonde hair. Another woman, leaning on the counter beside the kitchens, smiled and beckoned her over. They put their heads together and whispered. Under her starched white apron, the girl wore a short black rara skirt and scoop-neck black T-shirt. Her legs were the uniform tea colour of bottled tan, her breasts, bobbing over the top of her T-shirt, milk white. Clearly, she didn't get out much.

An cleared her throat. Reluctantly, Steve brought his gaze back to his dinner companion. 'Come on,' he said, handing her a bowl, 'let's see if you've learned the art of the salad bar yet.'

As she ripped the meat off a chicken wing with her teeth, he asked, 'So, Neets, what are your plans?'

'You sound like my father. "What are your plans for the future, An",' she mimicked. Steve crunched whitebait and waited.

'Well, I'll spend the summer at the homestead, more or less. Me and my mate Eloise might go camping for a couple of weeks. Devon or somewhere . . . What's so funny? I'm a real outdoors type now, you know. Yes,' she wagged a greasy finger at him. 'There's a lot you don't know about me.'

'And will I see you?'

'Of course you will.' She was surprised. 'Why wouldn't you?'

Steve shook his head, dismissing the question. 'I've got a mate down south, as it goes. Plymouth. Maybe I could go and visit him, we could all meet up. Is your mate pretty?'

She laughed, nearly said, 'Is your mate a woman?' but it was a bit soon for offering up secrets.

'How about you; going anywhere nice?'

'Might.' Steve picked at his teeth. 'It depends if Evi . . . if everyone at work, you know, can agree dates and that.' He took a long swig of his lager, his face hidden from her by the glass.

An studied him, covertly. It was such a relief to be with him. To feel that the pieces of her life were finally fitting into place; not just with Steve but with Beth. At last things were working out the way she'd hoped they would. She looked down at her plate, shyly. 'It's been really . . . you know, getting back together again. Even better than it was before. I know we haven't been able to spend much time and everything. In some ways it might be easier when I go back to Poly. Sheffield's no distance on the train, you can come at weekends. I've got a room in this amazing house, you'd love it, and the people I share with are brilliant.' An glanced at him and away again quickly. 'I've told them all about you.'

They finished their lager and ordered two more, plus medium steaks and french fries for the main course. An pushed her salad bowl aside and leaned across the table to sweep a piece of speared carrot through Steve's Thousand Island dressing.

Steve considered her, chewing over his words carefully. 'Have you been with . . . you're not still, like, a virgin, are you, Neets?'

She lowered her head, whispering, 'That was all over with the first time we met, don't you remember?'

'A virgin for me, kind of thing. I mean, I'd be surprised if you hadn't met someone at college. Gorgeous girl like you. You don't have to tell me, of course, I just wondered.' Steve dabbed at his mouth, laughing. He had turned a deep, strangled-looking shade of red, and seemed unable to meet her eye. 'You're kidding me, Neets. You must have a boyfriend.'

'Of course I have.'

'Thank God for that. For a minute there I thought I was in trouble.'

'Maybe you know him. Name of Stein.'

He reached through the crockery and took her hand. She snatched it away, suddenly wary.

'What?'

'What do you mean, "what"?' Steve threw up his hands and shrugged. So innocent looking.

'Why did you ask me that, about boyfriends? You want me to be seeing someone else, don't you?'

Steve inhaled deeply. 'Neets, I just want to know where your head is at. I think we've been operating at cross purposes these past few weeks. You know, a lot has changed. You can't really imagine that I've been sitting around twiddling my thumbs. Life has moved on since you left.'

'Just tell me.'

'I'm seeing someone else. Actually, I'm living with someone.'

An's thoughts reeled. He'd been sleeping with her, and living with another woman? So what did that make her? Mistress? Whore? A fool, for one thing. No wonder he could hardly spare the time to see her. An remembered the hotel room and felt the blood rush up in her face. He'd been screwing her over all along and she'd thought it was *love*. And what the hell had that tape been about, then, the love songs, Miles Jaye, for god's sake? Was that his idea of a joke? She felt something tugging at her, threatening at the edge of her consciousness. Greta would have spat in his face. No, she'd have got up from her chair, cooly, smilingly, and tipped her lager over his head. *Then* she would have spat in his face, turned the table over, turned the whole damn stinking corny place upside down. An clenched her hands and willed herself back, resisting. Steve wasn't worth it. He'd taken her to the brink of madness once. She wouldn't go there again for him. Not now. As suddenly as the rage had surfaced it subsided, to leave her feeling weak and used up and stupid.

'A woman?'

'No, a sheep. Of course a woman, Ani'a.'

She sat back in her chair and folded her arms. 'Now you sound like my mother.' She felt herself beginning to pout.

'Neets, look maybe I should have told you before. Christ, this is . . .' Steve rubbed his hands over his eyes and sighed. 'I'm a total shit, I know. I just wanted to see you again and I didn't know how to tell you. About her. Anyway, it's your fault too. You can't just disappear for years on end and expect to pick up where we left off. Of course I wanted to sleep with you. Sex with you is . . . I mean, it's the best. I wanted . . .'

People at neighbouring tables were beginning to look. She interrupted, 'Tell me about her, then.'

'Weeell.' Steve hesitated, giggling. 'Well, she's a year older than me, twenty-nine. She's white. She's Jewish. We met at Leicester. She was in my group on the CSW. What else do you want to know?' He didn't look at An. He looked up at the ceiling and twirled his eyes around. He squirmed in his seat and giggled again. 'She's little, a lot littler than me. She's got long dark hair. She thinks she's fat, but she's not really. She's got a laugh like a drain.'

Suddenly he remembered An, sitting bolt upright in her chair, eyes fixed on her lap.

'Her name's Evelyn,' he finished quietly. 'Evi. We call her Evi. She was with my mum, at the hospital, when my dad died. I was in the dayroom having a cigarette.' He shook his head.

The waitress arrived with the steaks. She put down An's plate, turned her back to her and, bending low over the table, presented Steve with his dinner. He blushed again. Coughing he said, 'Lovely. That's lovely.' The girl straightened. She pulled down her skirt at the back, smiling broadly. Very slowly, she walked back to the kitchens. Just as she got to the doorway she glanced over her shoulder and smirked at An. From far away, An heard Greta's whisper: 'Is that it? You're going to let him off playing the sympathy card? And feeling like cock-of-the-walk because some tart's practically lying down under him. . .' An shook her head, silencing the voice. It was no good. She couldn't do things Greta's way anymore, even if she had wanted to. She was, after all, only herself. Right now that didn't feel like much, but maybe she could muster a little bit of self-respect.

'They blamed you, you know.'

'Pardon me?'

'My parents. Daddy especially. I was good before I met you; stayed at home, studied hard, never said boo to a goose. If it hadn't been for you I would have passed my A levels. I wouldn't have got into all those fights with my dad. I might not have . . .' she caught herself sounding petulant. 'I'm going to slap that stupid girl in a minute.'

'What on earth are you talking about?'

An rolled her eyes up in her head. She picked up her steak knife and began to saw at the meat. A little pool of blood and meat juices began to gather in the bottom of her plate, staining the chips russet. Chewing, she said, 'So what are your plans then, Stevie?'

'Right now,' he said crossly, 'I'm going for a slash.'

'It's ridiculous. How the hell am I meant to react?'

'Bastard.'

'Cockney bastard. The worst thing is he agrees. Oh, he's coming clean now, all right. "I'm so sorry, Neets. It's just you're so sexy, Neets, I couldn't help myself. The thought of doing it with you again was too much for me."'

'He never said that!' Dap's mouth fell open. She nearly dropped the six-pack she was taking from the fridge.

'Of course he didn't. But almost. That's what he meant, anyway.'

'Cockney bast . . .'

An was tiring of the phrase. It had punctuated their rant for the past hour. The meal with Steve had ended in strained silence. As they left the restaurant she had suddenly remembered Dap's phone number, tucked into her purse. She had practically run away from Steve in her haste to get to a phonebox and onto the tube. Right at that moment, there was no one else on earth she wanted to talk to more. She just knew that Dap, of all people, would listen and not judge her.

'The funny thing is,' An broke in, 'he never even hit the spot. Not once.'

Dap looked bemused. She prised the lid off a bottled lager, then she realised what An meant. 'Oh. Ohhhh! Really? So what was the attraction then?'

An stopped pacing and stood in the middle of the room. The painted floorboards were cool under her bare feet. She looked down at her toes, wriggling about almost of their own volition, and shrugged. 'Dunno. He was the first, the first one that I wanted. The only one. That's all.'

Dap took a long swig of her drink and snorted. 'Well I think he's a git. D'you remember, I never could understand why he pronounced his name Steen instead of Stine? I still reckon he's not really Jewish, he just made it up to give himself street cred. A shameless ruse to get into your knickers, if you ask me.'

An said, 'What about that silly rhyme we made up?'

'Stevie Stein, Stevie Stein, Stevie Stein of Bethnal Green,' they shouted in unison, and laughed and laughed until Dap realised An wasn't laughing any more. Actually she was gasping, gulping like somebody drowning. She threw back her head and appealed to the ceiling, her voice high and out of control.

'Christ, Dap, what's wrong with me? Why am I always being punished? Don't I deserve something, a bit of love, something? I don't think I can take much more. . .'

Dap sat down on a beanbag, bottle in one hand, opener in the other. She never knew what to do in situations like this. An, with her arms limp at her sides, letting the tears fall, not even trying to cover her mouth. Just standing there with her face wet and shiny and twisted up. Dap looked away. In a little while she heard An sniff and blow her nose. She proffered the bottle and smiled.

An squatted down beside the futon and eased herself onto the floor. Her leg was starting to play up again. She pressed it discreetly through the fabric of her jeans.

'Do you want me to do that?'

Surprised, An stuttered, 'It's OK. Really.'

'Lie down,' Dap ordered. She took the lager from An and arranged her into a straight line beside her. 'Relax, I'm good at this.' Dap's chunky hand began to knead expertly at her thigh. 'Mmmn. You're all tensed up.' An winced as her friend's fingers found a particularly tender spot. Dap shook her head, tutting softly.

'So, Nita. What else is new?'

'Your place, for a start. It's lovely, Dap. These dark green boards are daring.' She tapped the floor. 'Very striking with – what colour do you call the walls?'

'Pumpkin.' Dap shuffled across the floor on her knees and picked up one of An's feet. Propping it on her upper leg, she placed her thumbs in the middle of the sole and began to stroke outwards with firm movements. 'Mmmmn,' she said again. Into the silence that followed came the click of the CD player, readying itself to sing. Earl Klugh and Bob James. The music poured into the room like water. Like balm. An closed her eyes and gave herself up to Dap's manipulations.

She must have dozed off. She became aware of Dap moving around the room, changing the light from sharp to subtle as she clicked lamps on in discreet corners. There was the scrape and hiss of a match. An opened her eyes to see Dap lighting the bunch of joss sticks stuck into a crack in the disused fireplace. She lay still as her friend tiptoed out.

The smell of sandalwood drifted round the room. It was nice lying on the floor. In the dim light, the room's strong colours were muted and the pot plants cast huge shadows across the walls. The ceiling seemed to recede into infinity. An turned her head sleepily and was startled to see two bright globes of light glistening at her from behind the futon. It was a cat; what looked like a huge fluffy tom, broad-nosed and big-pawed. An chirruped softly. The cat miaowed in reply but didn't move.

'So you've found Timmy, then?' Dap plopped down on the floor beside her and produced an old tobacco tin. From it she took Rizlas, loose tobacco and a little ball of something wrapped in Clingfilm. 'D'you remember him? He's the same one Ma gave me when I was twelve.' She began to crumble the stuff from the Clingfilm over a line of tobacco. 'We weren't sure if he'd accept the move but I couldn't live without you, could I, Timmy-kins?' Dap leaned forward and smooched the cat. Timmy-kins purred and closed his eyes.

'Roll this for me, will you?' She handed An the open spliff

and began to repeat the procedure on a new one. 'I may as well do all of this. Save me having to do it later.'

When she had rolled and lit it, An lay back down on the floor and closed her eyes. She held the smoke in her mouth and let it out slowly. It wreathed up into the air in thin streams from her mouth and nose. She coughed. Eyes watering, she handed the spliff back.

'Novice!'

'Easy nah, Sis. Cool runnings,' An replied, in a risible Jamaican accent. She raised her head and shook imaginary locks.

'Rastafari!'

'Oh, that reminds me of this time in the park.' An sat up eagerly. 'Stevie said . . .'

'Stevie said?' Dap blew smoke in her face. Still holding the spliff she reached out an index finger and pushed An gently in the chest. She gave her a long considered look. Closing one eye she delicately picked a shred of tobacco off the end of her tongue. 'That's very interesting. Now lie down; I haven't finished with you yet.'

It was the massage to end all massages. An felt like a pool of mercury. She half expected to slip through the floorboards. It would have been quite pleasant to lie underneath the floor, down amongst the dust and fluff, insubstantial, insignificant, and listen to Dap go about her daily business. She smiled.

'All done.' A mere whisper, tickling her ear. Dap's lips brushed her temple. She smoothed her hands over An's shoulders for the last time and shook her fingers to dissipate the tension. An imagined it floating away into the smoke-filled air. All gone. She was covered in a slick layer of scented oil that began to cool in the breeze from the open window. It felt as if a little lake of lavender and sweet almond was rippling in the small of her back. Then the light pressure of Dap's hand swept over her buttocks and up to her shoulder blades.

'Overdid it a bit.' Dap was still whispering.

The CD player hummed, ticked, and began to play track one of the Klugh and James again. 'Two of a Kind', that was it. It reminded An of a long night drive through Cornwall, with Eloise last summer. They had arrived in Polperro at about two o'clock. The town was wrapped in a milky veil of mist. The headlamps of the car made strange yellow shapes against the buildings. Eloise had driven down twisting streets and narrow lanes until they came to the sea. There, unable to see, they had gazed into the greyness while the music swelled and rolled around them. She had been exquisitely happy.

'You must meet my friend Eloise,' she mumbled. But Dap was already out of the room. She was back in a moment, holding a large bath towel.

She laid it gently across An's shoulders, as if putting a baby to bed. 'Come, sit up. You'll get a chill.'

An sat cross-legged while Dap rubbed at her through the coarse towelling. She was completely undone. Her head nodded and her eyes began to droop. They sat for a long time without speaking.

'Can I stay the night? With you?'

'Uh, sure. No probs. I'll pull the futon out.'

Dap spoke in a loud, jaunty voice. An looked up and stared at her as if seeing her for the first time. Dap's face was pale as sand. Her features were soft; a nose like a sweet dough ball and pink rosebud lips pushing out from a wide mouth. She had huge cowlike eyes, thick fringed with lashes; and perfect, crescent-shaped eyebrows which now arched questioningly.

'No. I mean with you, Dap. With you.'

Dap started to say something, to protest. An took her hands in both of hers, as Dap had done that evening at the homestead. When she had seen her oldest friend again after years of not even realising she had missed her.

They agreed. It wasn't a sex thing. They wriggled under the sheets and lay on their sides, gazing at each other. They had not agreed what kind of a thing it was. Then Dap reached over and kissed her. She kissed her eyes, her nose, both cheeks. She reached under the covers and brought out An's hands and kissed her fingers, each one in turn. Finally, she kissed her on the mouth. An let her lips be soft; a proper kiss, with tongues, but curiously chaste. Dap stretched out a hand and pulled the cord for the bedside lamp. The room darkened with the orange glow of the security lamps visible outside the bedroom window.

In the night, An wakened and felt Dap's breasts pillowed against her back and Dap's arms around her. She couldn't remember the last time she'd felt so comforted.

22

Bernard and the Cloth Monkey

'Lisa! Anita!'

You wake at the sound of your name. You were dreaming of shadows and danger.

'Lord, help me. Somebody call the police.'

The dark bursts in black bubbles before your eyes, your nightmare, you've brought it with you. Mummy's voice screams high then deep in her throat, strangled. You lie in the bed, sheets gripped to your chest, squinting at the light blaring in from the hallway.

'No, B. B, stop.'

You snap your head round towards the familiar shape in the bed in the corner. Empty, bedclothes trailing to the floor. You are alone, left behind outside the hurricane, hearing the crash and the chaos; always the last to know why.

'Please, B, you're ruining my neck, you're hurting me.'

Mustn't cry, not a drop. Have to see, find out what this terrible danger is that makes Mummy squeal and grunt. Then you hear the thumps and know it's a body hitting the wall again and again. Mummy's and Daddy's door smashes open and you're leaping back into the corner, trying to find a safe place. A scream goes up from Lisa and Greta who must be out on the landing. A flurry of movement. Brown legs and arms, scraps of floral nightie, pink hair rollers, faces like masks – they seem to dance in the narrow hallway, spinning away from the blast of rage that blows Mummy out of her room and half over the stair rail.

Now they are all here – except for Daddy – bundling through the doorway, puppet-show silhouettes on the bedroom wall. Mummy heaves and chokes. Clutching her torn nightie to her throat with one hand she throws an empty suitcase on your bed with the other.

Lisa clings to her, her voice is reedy thin. 'Mummy, Mummy, please don't go, don't go, Mummy, please.'

'I can't stay in this house a minute longer, I'm sorry. He'll murder me.' She drags out the spare clothes that she keeps in your wardrobe, cramming them into the case, higgledy-piggledy. All summer clothes. It's only March – she'll freeze, wandering through the streets of London with nowhere to go in just a cotton frock.

'Lisa-Beth,' her voice grates. She forces each word out as if it's got edges – serrated, like the bread knife. 'Get my tooth-brush and flannel from the bathroom. Put them in the striped washbag. And some underwear and a towel from the airing cupboard. Any towel! It doesn't matter. Now quickly.'

Greta stands by the door, not looking, not helping. Greta always knows what to do. Why won't she help?

Mummy looks up for the first time and sees you hiding in the corner. Her face is tear-stained and blotchy, one eye is closed, her lower lip juts out easily an inch over her chin. You don't know that face; you begin to whimper. Now your tears are falling. She lowers her gaze and puts her clenched hands to her head as if she is praying.

Lisa comes back with the toiletries and the underwear. She is shaking. Hurriedly Mummy snaps shut the case, stands and opens her arms. Lisa rushes to their shelter. Greta turns her face to the wall. You can't move, and Mummy lets her hand drop, useless, to her side. Lisa is trying not to scream. Her voice is a distant muffled siren. Mummy says, 'Sssh, girls, quiet now. Neighbours.'

'When will you come back?'

'When I can. When your father leaves me alone.' She pulls away and comes to lean over the bed. She kisses you, carefully, just above your hairline. You don't recognize the feel of her mouth.

'Take us with you.'

Greta looks up. She touches Mummy on the arm. 'Yes, take us with you.'

'I can't, baby,' Mummy strokes your hair, once, and turns to go. You do not follow her. You stay in your lonely places, where she has left you. You listen to the suitcase banging down the stairs. You hear the rustle and zip as she struggles into her coat and boots. Finally, the click of the door as she steps out into the night.

Daddy appears, bending over the stair rail, belligerent in striped pyjamas. 'And good riddance you frigid fucking bitch. Don't bother show your face here again, d'you hear me? We don't want you.'

You almost miss the gentle rattle of the door as it shuts behind her.

*   *   *

'Hardly a day goes by without me thinking of her. The first time I tried to separate from her, after the abuse ended, it felt really good to be just me again. Then I met Steve. God, that whole time was a roller-coaster. I was totally overwhelmed with everything I was thinking and feeling. I needed her again. So when she finally went it was like I was dead too. Every time I looked in the mirror I saw her face staring back at me. Once I even tried to . . .'

An cushioned her mug in the duvet, balancing it between her raised knees, and touched a finger to a thin scar on the side of her face. About an inch long, running along the ridge of her jawbone. Dap stared; she had never noticed it before. She shuddered. What a gruesome thing to do to yourself.

'It was a long time ago.' An laughed, mirthlessly. 'It hurt too badly. I guess I was still very much alive. I was sure I was dead, though. I felt as though I was dead.' She picked up her mug and sipped gingerly at the scalding chamomile tea.

Beside her in the bed, Dap folded her hands around her hot cup and rocked from side to side on her buttocks. This talk of Greta was making her nervous. She could feel her mind racing ahead, full of question. When, why, how, what was it *like*? She opened her mouth to speak and shut it again. No, that wouldn't be fair. That was the kind of thing Claudette might do. Quizzing people, fascination and repulsion glittering in her eyes. But Dap owed An more than that. They used to be so close it had become part of their personal mythology. Anytime, she'd said. You can talk about Greta to me anytime. Well then, here they were.

Dap looked at her friend's thin shoulders and her ebony profile, stark against the bright mid-morning light. She was like a bird. A sad bird, but somehow indomitable, like an eagle.

When they were little it was always Nita leading. Nita who knew what to say and do, where to go, which friends to make and which to leave. Nita showed her the latest games, told the newest jokes, always put her hand up first in class. Nita was dark as Dap's shadow, but it was Dap who had been in the shade. It was warm there and exciting. She had not wanted it any other way.

By the time Nita told her about the Island, and the things her Daddy made her do there, Nita had changed. She had grown paler, less solid, less sure of herself. Then Dap was moved to another class, and later they went to different schools; the inseparable 'twins' had been separated. First by primary-school administration and then by ability. But they still talked, when they could. They trusted each other. Nita was the only one who knew how Dap felt about her new best friend. So it was fair that Dap should be the only one to know about the Island.

So many years. She wondered how things would have turned out if they had stayed close. And what about Beth? Less than a year older than An they were as near in age as siblings who aren't twins can be. Perhaps there would have been no need for Greta if An had had someone she could rely on. If An was a different kind of person now – weaker, more damaged, a victim – it would be tragic. Dap put her mug on the bedside table and draped an arm around An's shoulders.

An stared at her, a baited look in her eye. 'Can I tell you something, Dap? A secret, a really terrible one.'

Dap held her breath.

'Sometimes,' whispered An, 'she haunts me, and I want her to go back. Back to where she came from.'

'Haunts you?'

'I know she was never real. I know I made her up but she was part of me for so long, sometimes I can see her, smell her, feel her. She used to come whenever I was angry or desperate about something. If I get like that now, I still wish she would come. I can deal with that part of it. I talk about it in therapy and the need gets less and less all the time. But sometimes I wonder. I wonder if she was real, like I was possessed or something. And I get so scared that she might come back without me calling her. And take me over so I'd be Greta, not An. And no-one would ever know the difference.'

Dark, too dark, can't sleep when it's dark like this, switch the light on please for the love of God I need to sleep, sleep in heavenly peace swinging low sweet charioteer coming for me

You knew she wouldn't leave you not after all you've been through together from the start curled like ying and yang snug in each other belly to belly two peas. Must have been warm then. Safe and still. One has to keep swimming and flailing felt as feet and elbows trying to break out. That's what the women say and pat their stomachs like the memory is there held in folds of brown skin. But two now twins! Two float without fighting two are glad of confinement two still or some-times ripple bobbing gently in the water like a ball of light light as ether . . . there . . . gone. Eternal peace heavenly peace at the start and at the close of day. So tired all you want to do is close your eyes but then you see red and explosions and if you wait till all the noise in your eyes goes away like they tell you to *just relax, relax that's right* she's there with Pierrot's sad smile lit up behind her. Like she's got two faces the black one turning flat expressionless on the bed like the life is drain-ing out of her as you watch though she must have been dead

for hours. And the white face with the thin lips and that big
tear endlessly dropping and the eyes fringed with grief saying
pity me or I will die of a broken heart. She's a star a ball of
light exploding to a star the air cracks and fizzes where she
passes the bed is bright with the fire of her. First she was
coiled tight as a fist around you and you stayed that way
whispering secrets but someone undid her stretched her limb
from limb and laid her flat five-pointed. They want for you
to see her stuck here here behind your eyes or maybe it's not
her anymore but a picture that someone's put there and if
you look at it long enough there's a third face. You told them
warned them about the third face lying next to hers on the
bed fading up through the quilt like a stain getting darker and
darker. *Look into the light* they say *embrace it* if only you could.
You would hold the light so tenderly cradle it croon it to sleep
scorch yourself on its fierceness till it reached up its arms and
held you too. Consumed in the fire consumed in the firma-
ment heavenly peace at last both of you burning brightly
turning to black etched shadows printed on the bed. Soot and
dust and no one can keep you now. Free at last. You don't
need their help their needles and cups their elixirs their locks.
How can they help you they know nothing at all they never
went to the Island never had to do the things you've had to
do make shelters with your bare hands and eat sea monsters
writhing in your stomach for days and days until you throw
it all up every last bit of it and start again. If they'd been to
the Island they'd know. Oh the whiteness of the sand the
blueness of the sea even the trees waving welcome and
the birds wheeling your name in sky writing. Writing it in the
clouds singing just for you. Such a beautiful place almost like
peace at first almost home except that night falls so quickly

and the eye of God turns the sea to blood. It sinks into the water and watches you it sees you stumble and cry and it winks and says not a soul remember clenching red fist inside your head. They say *that's right relax now look again slowly tell us what you see who is it what is her name.* And you say *don't know want to sleep for the love of God let me sleep.*

You won't tell them the third face is yours.

Beth's shadow hovered in the hallway as An walked up the garden path. She could see her sister's shape wavering through the glass, bits of her breaking up and reforming behind the metal grille.

'Where have you been? I was worried sick. Steve phoned.'

'What did he say?' An dropped her rucksack and jacket on the floor and sat at the foot of the stairs.

'Nothing, just to tell you he'd called. I thought you were with him. An, what's going on?'

She wasn't in the mood to go over it all again. She wasn't up to 'I told you so's. 'Look, I'm just going upstairs to put a dress on, it's scorching today isn't it?'

Beth thought she understood. 'I'm in the garden. I'll pour you some ginger beer.'

She had the photo albums out, spread across a blanket in the shade of the apple tree. Her yellow dress fanned out around her, revealing the tops of her legs. An flopped down next to her; the white cotton of her shift overlapped with the yellow. She leaned her head near to Beth's and their hair danced in the static electricity.

There was a picture of her and Daddy in the garden. It had been summer then, too. He'd been painting the front of the house, if she remembered rightly. Daddy in paint-spattered shirt, sun glinting off his bald patch, stared into the camera, a fixed smile on his face. A teenage An posed in a wicker chair beside him. Her eyes were hidden behind the twin discs of her spectacles. She had on a close-fitting cotton dress, low-cut and cap-sleeved. Her high chest stood out, chiselled by sun and shade, sculpted in floral fabric. Daddy rested one hand on her shoulder and his shadow fell across her lap.

'Jeez, I look awful in those glasses. They always made us wear real granny specs.'

'Better than those round ones with the curly arms. Used to near enough cut your ears off.'

'Thank God for contact lenses.'

'Yeah, the myopic Moore sisters.'

Beth turned the pages. Seaside trips, family Christmases, a holiday in Jamaica. An and Beth climbing Dunn's River Falls; sitting on a huge stone lion in the grounds of some stately home; playing in the grass outside a guest house in Ireland. They laughed about the clothes they wore. Beth, Miss Junior 1970s in striped hotpants and floppy hat. Beth and An with their arms around each other in matching suits: plaid jacket and trousers and frilly white blouses. In the photo hovered another little girl, younger than An, a fat bunch of hair on either side of her head, and orange handbag perched on her thin brown arm. They stood against a background of trees, trimmed to form a high hedge.

'Isn't that Michaela, Auntie Vi's youngest? I remember the handbag, I always wanted one like it. Where was that taken, then?'

'Hampton Court, I think.' Beth peered at the photograph. 'Yeah, outside the maze.'

An said, 'I was thinking about Michaela the other day. D'you remember, she had an imaginary friend? Little Michael. Auntie had to set an extra place at the table otherwise she'd have hysterics. Whatever happened to Little Michael? The funny thing is, I can see him, clear as day. In my mind's eye. A little boy looking just like Michaela, without the bunches. Isn't that strange?'

It was an awkward gambit. An wasn't really surprised when Beth ignored it. She herself was no longer sure what she wanted to talk about, or what she hoped to achieve. She did seem to have a way of getting Beth's back up. Maybe she should leave well alone, for now – wait till she had a session with her therapist. Sylvia would help her work it out.

They looked at the pictures again, in silence. On a Girls' Brigade day out. On a youth hostel trip with the church. As teenagers at a cousin's wedding.

The question An had been wanting to ask ever since she came home leapt into her mind and blurted out. 'Beth, whatever happened to George?'

'Chicken George?' Beth laughed, then shook her head sadly. 'I never told him, you know. About the abortion. He knew, though. Someone must have said something, probably his Mum. He never tried to contact me or anything and he would have if he thought his child was out there. After he came out of prison he moved away. Dette keeps her ear to the ground; she always seems to know what everyone we went to school with is up to. Last I heard, he was some big hard man up Birmingham way.'

'I'm sorry.'

'Yeah. Me too.'

An rolled onto her back and shaded her eyes with her hand. 'You know I was talking about going camping with Eloise?

I've persuaded Dap to come. I think they'd really hit it off. How'd you fancy making up a foursome?'

'What about the house, we can't just . . .'

'Mrs Golightly can keep an eye out. Come on, Beth. You deserve a proper holiday. We've never been away together, you know, without Mummy and Daddy or some other grown-ups.'

'Camping.' Beth measured the word, giving the two syllables full weight. 'I've never been camping before. Yeah, alright.' She giggled. 'Oooh. I can't wait.'

An smiled and closed her eyes. Friends. It would do for now. She and Beth would talk later, on holiday maybe. Things would settle down and Beth would open up and they'd be really close. Really, really close, like twins. All they needed was time.

The insides of her eyelids glowed red. She could see all the little veins making spidery black lines, twitching and swarming against the hot background. Then she saw herself, dragging her body off the hall carpet and up the stairs. She couldn't remember feeling any pain or hearing any sound. It was like moving through a dream. She floated along the landing and through the bedroom door.

It changed every time she looked at it. Did it matter? Probably not. Greta was hers, had always been hers, to do with as she pleased. Pierrot lay crying in duplicate, smoothed out across the twin beds. This must be what dying's like, only in reverse. Here she was in the doorway, and here was her outline on the bed. Fading away now, fading away, bleaching out like a stain. Only the white face left with the thin lips and that big tear, endlessly dropping, and the eyes fringed with grief, saying 'pity me'.

Marsha Hunt

Like Venus Fading

'A tragic, sometimes brutal story told with the delicacy of an angel's breath'   *Irish Independent*

'Irene O'Brien is a fictional black Marilyn Monroe who cheats her own death, fakes suicide, and finds a happy posthumous life as a woman reborn. Gaining control of her destiny, she belies the labels that ought to hang around her neck: the victim of poverty, of sexual abuse and of being born black . . . Marsha Hunt writes keenly of the things that clutter everybody's life, and Irene's story subtly becomes a universal one of intimate identity and troublesome family bonds.'

ROGER CLARKE, *Mail on Sunday*

'A deeply moving novel that tells the shocking story of a beautiful black woman, abused as a child, abused as a wife and abused by the Hollywood star system when she becomes the first black screen goddess in 1950s Hollywood . . . Yet, *Like Venus Fading* is also a heartbreaking story of emancipation and, ultimately, of hope.'

JACKIE McGLONE, *Scotland on Sunday*

flamingo

Ferdinand Dennis

Duppy Conqueror

Marshall Sarjeant is born in Paradise, Jamaica. As a young man, he is entrusted with a mystical quest, to overcome a curse that has been put on his family. To do this he must return to Africa, whence his ancestors were brought as slaves.

Marshall's journey takes him first to wartime London, where he marries and mixes with a clubland crowd of musicians and politicians, and then on to Africa and the struggle to escape from the colonial past.

Eventually he returns to Paradise to confront the duppy, or ghost, that started him on his voyage.

In the telling of Marshall's story, Ferdinand Dennis has created a powerful narrative of the African experience, and in its breadth of vision and feeling a novel that is truly universal.

'An ambitious and compelling novel . . . bubbling with eccentric characters and poetic descriptions . . . packed to the brim with layers of symbolism, individual and cultural memories, and fascinating historical stories. Reading it once won't be enough'   *Independent*

'This novel may well prove a landmark in British fiction in capturing a breadth of diasporic experience and a moment in empire. Its haunting mythologising of migration seeks to make of a bafflingly complex and often painful journey something luminous and redemptive'   *Guardian*

ISBN 0 00 649784 5

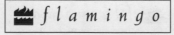

Arundhati Roy

The God of Small Things

THE INTERNATIONAL NO 1 BESTSELLER
WINNER OF THE 1997 BOOKER PRIZE

'They all crossed into forbidden territory, They all tampered with
the laws that lay down who should be loved, and how. And how
much.'

'From its mesmerising opening sequence, it is clear that we
are in the grip of a delicious new voice . . . a voice of breath-
taking beauty. *The God of Small Things* achieves genuine,
tragic resonance. It is, indeed, a masterpiece.'

                                      CHRISTINA PATTERSON, *Observer*

'The joy of *The God of Small Things* is that it appeals equally to
the head and the heart. It is clever and complex, yet it makes
one laugh, and finally, moves one to tears. A masterpiece,
utterly exceptional.'

                         WILLIAM DALRYMPLE, *Harpers & Queen*

'A compelling story which somehow marries the deepest,
smallest personal emotions with an epic narrative. There
were times I had to stop reading this novel because I feared so
much for the characters, or I had to re-read a phrase or a page
to memorise its grace.'   **MEERA SYAL**, *Daily Express*

'It is rare to find a book that so effectively cuts through the
clothes of nationality, caste and religion to reveal the bare
bones of humanity. A sensational novel.'

                               CLAIRE SCOBIE, *Daily Telegraph*

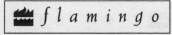

Meera Syal

Anita and Me

'A marvellous crash course in Asian/Brummie culture. Funny, moving and packed full of wonderful surprises.'

ESTER FREUD

Like every nine-year-old girl, Meena can't wait to grow up and break free from her parents. But, as the daughter of the only Punjabi family in the mining village of Tollington, her fight for independence is different from most.

Meena wants fishfingers and chips, not just chapati and dhal; she wants an English Christmas, not the interminable Punjabi festivities she has to attend with her embarrassing Aunties and dreadful cousins, Pinky and Baby – but more than anything, more than mini-skirts, make-up and the freedom to watch *Opportunity Knocks*, Meena wants to roam the backyards of working-class Tollington with the feisty Anita Rutter and her gang . . .

With great warmth and brilliantly observed dialogue, Meera Syal creates a superb cast of characters, from the wise and devious old Nanima to the curious Mr Worrall, stranded in his front room since the war. Written with extraordinary grace and charm, and just a hint of wistfulness, *Anita and Me* is a unique vision of a British childhood in the Sixties, a childhood caught between two cultures, each on the brink of enormous change.

'A wonderful book – very funny and very moving. *Tom Sawyer* meets *Cider With Rosie* en route to India via Wolverhampton. Treat yourself.'

BEN ELTON

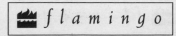